June 6, 2014

To the Incoming Class of 2014.

Dear Incoming Student,

Welcome to this special edition of Cary Fagan's collection of stories, *My Life Among the Apes*. Each story is independent of the others but there is, to my mind, a broad recurring theme. Of course, you will draw your own conclusions. And, as part of the joys of university life, I am sure that your initial thoughts will be richly refined and amplified through discussion with your classmates and professors in the Common Reading Program.

I love to read, and I read a lot. The act of reading is both a solitary activity and a shared experience. We read to ourselves, silently engaged with the text, oblivious to the hustle and bustle of the world around us, and yet we are not alone. At the very least, we are spending time with the author and his or her ideas and characters. But, in truth, we have joined an even larger group. Nearly everything we read has been read by others, and in this respect the solitary act of reading engages us in a much wider community.

The shared experience of reading is a fundamental and delightful part of academic life. It provides a platform for exploring new ideas and different points of view with professors and students. At its very best, the process of discussing what we read is a stimulating and inspiring way to acquire knowledge, gain insights and develop our own thoughts.

The intent of Laurier's Common Reading Program is to introduce you to the wonderful world of shared experience of learning in the university setting. You are among more than

1,400 first-year Faculty of Arts students who are encouraged to read *My Life Among the Apes* over the summer and, when you arrive on campus in September, to engage in a wide variety of activities designed to explore and enhance this shared experience.

Congratulations on taking part in what I am certain will be an enjoyable, stimulating, and personally rewarding experience to begin your student life with us a Laurier. I would also like to thank the many faculty and staff at Laurier who worked hard to bring the Common Reading Program to life.

Sincerely,

D.Max Blouw, PhD
President and Vice-Chancellor

Faculty of Arts Common Reading Program
Incoming Class of 2014
Wilfrid Laurier University

June 6, 2014

Dear Incoming Student:

Welcome to Laurier! As a new student in the Faculty of Arts on the Waterloo campus, you have a wonderful opportunity to engage in our Common Reading Program, which this year features Cary Fagan's *My Life Among the Apes*. This book was especially chosen for you by the Faculty of Arts from a long list of contenders.

I was thrilled to learn that a book of short stories was the chosen common book. I love short stories because they involve the reader quickly and — often in a very few pages — tell unforgettable tales that can cover a time span as short as an afternoon or a week, or as long as a life time. Cary Fagan's *My Life Among the Apes* doesn't disappoint. It contains characters and settings that on one hand are very familiar because they are recognizably "Canadian" but at the same time are totally unique, with characters that stay with the reader long after the stories are finished.

Whether you consider yourself "a reader" or not, I'm sure that you'll find much to appreciate in this collection. I hope that you will choose to read this terrific Canadian book over the summer and that you take the opportunities that will be provided in the fall to discuss the short stories with your fellow students and professors. By reading the same book, the Common Reading Program will give you a way to connect immediately and form a community with others at Laurier as soon as you arrive.

Enjoy your summer! We look forward to welcoming you to Laurier and the Common Reading Program in the fall.

*[signature]*

Deborah MacLatchy, PhD
Vice-President: Academic & Provost

Faculty of Arts Common Reading Program
Incoming Class of 2014
Wilfrid Laurier University

June 6, 2014

Dear Incoming Student:

This year the book chosen for our Common Reading Program is Cary Fagan's *My Life Among the Apes*. This collection of short stories is being sent to every first-year student in the Faculty of Arts, with the hope that you will read these stories over the summer and bring the book with you in September, when you'll get a chance to meet the author in person.

When we discussed this book in the Selection Committee (a committee composed of students, faculty and staff) we found that different members had different favourite stories and focused on different themes. For me, this collection is about dreams — what happens when you pursue your dreams, what happens when you don't, and the gains and losses that can come with either scenario. I look forward to hearing how these stories connect with you.

Those of us in the Dean's Office hope that this shared reading experience, as well as the discussions and other events that will take place surrounding it at the beginning of the school year, will add to that sense of community for which Laurier is known. It will make your first few weeks at Laurier even more memorable.

I look forward to seeing you when you arrive on campus.

All the best,

*Mike*

Mike Carroll
Dean, Faculty of Arts

# MY LIFE AMONG THE APES

## STORIES BY

## CARY FAGAN

*Cormorant Books*

Canada Council
for the Arts
Conseil des Arts
du Canada
 ONTARIO ARTS COUNCIL
CONSEIL DES ARTS DE L'ONTARIO
an Ontario government agency
un organisme du gouvernement de l'Ontario

Canadian   Patrimoine
Heritage   canadien
Canadä

The publisher gratefully acknowledges the support of the Canada Council
for the Arts and the Ontario Arts Council for its publishing program.
We acknowledge the financial support of the Government of Canada
through the Canada Book Fund (CBF) for our publishing activities, and
the Government of Ontario through the Ontario Media Development
Corporation, an agency of the Ontario Ministry of Culture,
and the Ontario Book Publishing Tax Credit Program.

LIBRARY AND ARCHIVES CANADA CATALOGUING IN PUBLICATION

Fagan, Cary
My life among the apes / Cary Fagan.

Short stories.
Issued also in electronic formats.
ISBN 978-1-77086-087-2

I. Title.

PS8561.A375M88 2012   C813'.54   C2012-900266-6

Cover photograph and design: Angel Guerra/Archetype
Interior text design: Tannice Goddard, Soul Oasis Networking
Printer: Trigraphik LBF

Printed and bound in Canada.

 MIX
Paper from
responsible sources
FSC® C107923
www.fsc.org

The interior of this book is printed on 30% post-consumer waste recycled paper.

CORMORANT BOOKS INC.
390 Steelcase Road East, Markham, Ontario, L3R 1G2
www.cormorantbooks.com

*To Rebecca,*
*for the best story*

# Contents

The Floating Wife 1

Shit Box 13

I Find I Am Not Alone on the Island 35

Wolf 49

My Life among the Apes 67

The Creech Sisters 81

The Brooklyn Revenge 95

Dreyfus in Wichita 113

Lost at Sea 133

The Little Underworld of Edison Wiese 155

Acknowledgements 191

"He felt as a conjurer must who is all the time afraid that at any moment his tricks will be seen through."

— Tolstoy, *War and Peace*

# MY LIFE AMONG
# THE APES

# The Floating Wife

MY HUSBAND, ALBERT NATHAN ZARETSKY, was, until his retirement, a judge of the Supreme Court of Ontario. Before his bench were heard the most grave criminal and civil accusations in the province, while the most sensational cases were written about in the newspapers and reported on the television news. He was famous (or notorious, depending on one's position) for allowing Charter arguments to be made and unusual precedents to be cited, and his decisions were appealed before the Supreme Court of Canada more often than most. He looked good on television, for he was a handsome man even in his late years when his hair was still full but absolutely white, and his slightly large features — his prominent eyebrows, his heavy pocked nose, his sensual lips — became more so as his face grew thinner. Actually, he was much more handsome as an older man; when I first saw him, a first-year law student, his head looked too big for his neck and his arms and legs too long.

But Albert had another life, one outside the legal profession. He belonged to a secretive world, what in other circumstances spouses most fear from their partners. In that world, my husband was known as Zardoff the Mysterious, not so much to the public but in magicians' circles, here in Toronto and also in New York and Los Angeles and, to a lesser extent, London. As a judge he was a forward-thinking champion of individual rights, but as a magician he was a strict traditionalist, eschewing modern technology in favour of the older and, in his opinion, more elegant methods of misdirection and sleight of hand.

I myself am not an expert (far from it), but by all accounts he was a steady performer, skilful without being outstanding. Some praised his stiff, rather formal presentation, while others criticized it. Of course, he could only practise for an hour or so a day after supper, and he performed only as an unpaid amateur (he refused a fee when one was offered) for Boy Scout troops, in hospital wards, and at charity functions. Yet he had, at least as well as I can understand, a fame in the conjuring world equal to his fame in the legal profession. This fame was not for his performances, but for his collection of Victorian and early twentieth-century conjuring apparatus. These objects, acquired at auctions and estate sales, often with the assistance of an agent, he had begun to accumulate in the late fifties, when it was still possible to find important pieces at reasonable prices. He owned a cabinet built for the Davenport brothers, Heller's second-known black art table, a pair of pistols used by Anderson in his version of the bullet-catching trick, Chung Ling Soo's miracle board vanish, and perhaps three hundred more effects, all stored in a museum-quality setting, in a special room built onto the back of the house, which had necessitated the removal of the original tennis court. My husband was famous not only for owning the collection, but for his knowledge of how the illusions were originally presented, and for his generosity in granting access. Magicians came from all over the world, strange men (they were almost always men) who would astonish our children by pulling watermelons out of their ears.

I remember one occasion in the early seventies when, by an accident of scheduling, the premier of the province, who wanted Albert to head a commission on payoffs in the building trades, arrived in a limousine at our house for tea at the same time that Robert Harbin, the creator of the zig-zag girl illusion, arrived by cab from the airport. I answered the door to the both of them and was highly embarrassed, but my husband simply introduced the politician and the conjurer to one another and, after the premier swore an oath of secrecy, the three of them spent several hours in the special wing.

What I thought, standing alone in my kitchen: boys, they're still and always boys. You must understand that I hated magic. The ridiculous names (Zardoff, for God's sake), the black capes and top hats and gimmicked canes, the hands that could never be still but always had to be producing cigarettes or "walking" coins over the knuckles. The arguments over the relative greatness of Le Roy and Devant, the inevitable shouting and finger pointing whenever Houdini's name came up. It was all so childish. As if there could be anything of interest in seeing a man scatter four aces in a deck only to find them in a spectator's pocket, or a woman in a leotard getting trussed up, shoved into a burlap bag, and locked into a trunk, only to appear a flashing moment later on top of the trunk itself, having changed places with the magician. Why did it matter that the magician had performed a false shuffle, or had used Maskelyne's method for releasing the chains? It was all child's play.

WHEN WE MET IN THE early fifties, Albert was not only attending classes but also holding down two jobs, one dipping ice cream bars at the Neilson plant on Spadina Avenue, the other shelving books at the law library. His parents had come from Galitzia and opened a small shoe store in Thunder Bay. Albert was living in a boarding house on Harbord Street run by a Mrs. Mossoff. He was so thin because Mrs. Mossoff put a small amount of the cheapest ground meat into her stews, which she poured over potatoes every night and which Albert often vomited up. In fact, on our first meeting, a blind date arranged by a mutual friend, we were walking down Yonge Street to see the Christmas display in the window of Eaton's when he collapsed on the sidewalk. I took him home to my mother's kitchen and fed him.

Back then, his head was full of ideas. He was in love with the law and revered the British legal system, which he saw as an antidote to the grotesque legal distortions enacted by the Nazis. We would go to Diana Sweets for coffee and pie and talk away the evening, Albert leaning forward, eyes aflame, a little spittle gathering at the corner of his mouth as his voice grew louder with excitement and I had to put my hand over his and gently hush him.

He was socially advanced for our time. He encouraged me to believe that, although he foresaw a future for us, he did not want me to restrict my life to that of a housewife. I was an undergraduate with some thought of becoming a nurse but half-expecting that my education and career would end in marriage. With Albert's emotional and financial support, I became not just a nurse but a doctor, one of the few women M.D.s in the province. I returned to work after each of our three children was born, Albert assuring me that I could be a good mother even if we needed a nanny to pick up the children from school.

When I first met him, Albert's interest in magic was a harmless pastime. He had become interested, he told me, upon discovering that an uncle on his mother's side had been a professional magician in Hamburg, Berlin, Budapest, and Prague. He had found a book at Britnell's (*The Amateur Magician's Handbook* by Henry Hay) and had learned a few simple but effective sleights that he showed to me one evening: making a card rise out of the deck, changing a red handkerchief to green, and so on. This was, I think, the only time I enjoyed watching him perform, mostly because of the pleasure that he himself clearly got out of it. But I was less pleased when, about a month later, we met in the Hart House Library and from his beaten-up briefcase he drew out a wooden box with two little doors. He opened one of the doors and put in a block of wood painted with spots like a die. When he opened the door, the die was gone; apparently it had slid behind the other door. But it wasn't behind that door either, for it had somehow jumped back into the briefcase. Three or four students in the library seemed to enjoy the little performance, but I was embarrassed and dismayed by it. Afterwards, Albert confided to me that he had just discovered a magic shop on Dundas Street and that he had spent a day's pay for the trick. I was going to say something, that I wondered if magic was a suitable interest for an adult, or perhaps that it would be better if he saved his money, but I didn't get the chance, because he suddenly got down on his knee, grasped my hand, and implored me to marry him.

ALBERT WAS NEVER, IN FORTY-THREE years of marriage, an unfaithful husband. He could easily have been, for women found him attractive even without the allure of his powerful position. I suspect that even if he had been tempted, he would have been too mindful of his robes to risk sullying the position he held. If he had been unfaithful, my leaving him would be more understandable, more justifiable to the outside world and to our children, who adored him.

I do not wish to spend a great deal of time recounting the details of his hobby-turned-obsession. The hours spent in the basement practising the linking rings, or donning his custom-made set of tails (tails!) to work at his silent dove act (he had a small aviary and, to the kids' delight when they were young, a rabbit hutch). Every magician who passed through town was welcome in our house, no matter the time of day. Often they were alcoholic; one used his skills to steal silver. At night in bed, Albert pored over catalogues from magical supply dealers and auction houses.

YOU MUST UNDERSTAND, I KNOW that my husband worked extremely hard at a job of tremendous pressure. He was an otherwise attentive husband and a good father, and he never wavered in his support of my own career as a doctor, a lecturer, and later the co-founder of a women's hospice. I would have stayed with him, no matter how sick I became of phrases such as "forcing," "penetration frame," and "coin clip," or how often at a dinner party he would unscrew the top of the salt shaker, pour the contents into his hand, and then throw it at the guest across the table only to have the salt vanish. I would have stayed if, after his retirement, he had not decided — no, insisted — on turning professional.

For several months he did not tell me that he had hired a director, a man who had worked with several established acts in Las Vegas and New York, to help him create a stage show. That he had found a 150-seat theatre to rent every Saturday night where he would perform as Zardoff the Mysterious. That he had found a young woman assistant who was lithe enough to fold herself into a basket or fit into that same zig-zag girl cabinet. (Many of my friends would assume that Albert was having an affair with the young woman, a common occurrence in the magic world.) When he did tell me I said no. I was absolutely clear about it, but perhaps he didn't believe me. Or he believed me but hoped that I would change my mind. Or believed me but decided to go ahead anyway. It was the last possibility that made me realize I could not change my mind even if I wanted to. And so, when he returned from opening night, I was gone.

I slept at the hospital for a few days, then a hotel, and then rented a condominium at Bay and Wellesley. Our kids, young adults by now, were angry at me. Especially our eldest son, who threatened to derail his plans to enter medical school, as if this was a way to get back at me. Our daughter, the middle one, kept her usual neutral stance, while the youngest boy decided to stay with me, although it meant a subway and bus trip to Forest Hill Collegiate every day.

I did not cut off all communication with Albert. We spoke on the phone for a few minutes every day, mostly about the kids but also about our work, never mentioning my having left or his magic show. I only knew it was still running from the entertainment listings. And then some anonymous "friend" sent me a review of the show in the weekly arts paper *Now*, with what intention I don't know. The review both mocked and praised Albert's solemn demeanour, but what caught my attention was the final paragraph.

*Zardoff (whose real name is nowhere listed in the program) seems to think that the world has not changed in a hundred years and that people can still be astounded by objects vanishing, endless coins pouring into a top hat, and "spirits" writing messages on chalk boards. He believes that a striking head, lit in profile and with one hand raised, can make an audience grow silent with expectation. And he is weirdly right, or nearly so. But nothing that comes before will prepare you for the show's pièce-de-résistance, the climactic illusion that he calls "The Floating Wife." I heard people laugh and, when the lights came up, I saw more than a few surreptitiously wiping tears from their eyes. As for me, I just wanted to know how the damn trick worked.*

Naturally I was dismayed and also possibly angry. How could I not be? Surely there were people in the audience on some nights who recognized Albert and knew me as well. It also occurred to me that, given Albert's nature, I ought to be flattered. And then I discovered that all three of our children had gone to see the show.

"I'm not going to describe it for you," my eldest son said on the phone. He was still refusing even to see where I lived. "It's no more nor less than you deserve. I think it would do you good to see it for yourself."

"I don't think Dad means anything by it," my daughter said. "It's just a good illusion, that's all. He probably wasn't even thinking of you."

"It's sweet," said my youngest at breakfast. "It's *so* Dad. Go and see it. I bet you'll cry and you don't cry easily."

It didn't seem as if I had much choice. Still, I waited another week before finally booking a ticket on the telephone, which meant leaving my name on the answering machine. I wondered whether Albert knew that I was coming, and even if he had created "The Floating Wife" expecting that I would see it. The theatre was in a decrepit building, a small, former chicken slaughterhouse. The seats had been rescued from a cinema that was being torn down to put up a multiplex. It was a little more than half full, but there was nobody I knew in the audience. At eight o'clock the curtain did not go up. Nor at eight-thirty. Finally the assistant came out from between the curtains, clearly distraught. My first thought was maybe they were having an affair after all. And then she announced that "Mr. Zardoff" had become ill just before coming to the theatre and had been taken to hospital.

It took me ten minutes to find a cab. I urged him to drive faster, but it did no good. Albert was already dead. He'd suffered a myocardial infarction — a heart attack. They were only just cleaning up the emergency room and he was still on the table. I have seen more than my share of corpses, but when you see the body of the man you have shared your life with you are no longer a doctor.

We had been separated but still husband and wife, and the funeral arrangements fell to me. I wouldn't have wanted it differently. The service was overflowing with friends, lawyers and judges and other members of the judicial system, the mayor, the premier and several cabinet ministers, people I didn't recognize. Everyone silently agreed to overlook the fact of our late separation. But what none of them knew was that an hour before the service, I had a terrible argument with both the rabbi and the director of the Jewish funeral home.

There is a tradition that when a magician dies, his wand is broken in half and ceremoniously thrown into the coffin with him. The rabbi and the director did not want to allow it. In the end, we compromised. I broke the wand (Albert had about two dozen, I just picked one) and placed it in the coffin before the service.

I LIVE IN THE FOREST HILL house again, a widow. Unlike Albert, I have chosen not to retire. My practice is busier than ever, given the current crisis in our health care system, and I have taken on extra teaching duties as well. Exhausted from the day, I go to bed almost as soon as I get home. Every so often the doorbell rings: a magician, visiting town, has come to see

Albert's collection. I let them in, telling them to see themselves out when they are done. Sometimes the magician will ask me about "The Floating Wife," an illusion that, as far as I can gather, has become something of a legend in conjuring circles. But of course, I can say nothing about it.

# Shit Box

I AM TRYING TO BALANCE the *New York Review of Books* on my lap while eating Kraft Dinner from a plastic bowl. Well, not actually Kraft Dinner, but a no-name imitation with cheese that is so intensely, unreally orange that it is almost fluorescent. I am struggling through an essay about the Armenian genocide that refers to several new books and also a film by Atom Egoyan. I used to know Atom when Candice and I went to a lot of Toronto parties and openings. I hadn't quite figured out what I was going to do: make films, write poems, or create some new cross-disciplinary form to capture the paradox of our late capitalist, terrorized, hypererotic Starbucks lives.

What I actually became was a pharmaceutical rep.

I roam from medical office to doctor's office with my square leather sample case, meeting doctors and suggesting to them that they prescribe our anti-depressant, our anti-inflammatory, our analgesic pain killer, our contraceptive pill, our alternative to Viagra (no hot flushes, no seeing purple). I load them up with free samples to hand out to patients — candy, we call them. My territory is the northern outskirts of Toronto: Markham, Thornhill, the 905 arc over the city, which I traverse like a voyageur for the good of the distant mother country, a massive German pharmaceutical corporation. The job was supposed to be temporary. Candice was already working as a lawyer for the province and I felt bad every time we went to a restaurant and she took out her Visa. What I think happened, what I can reconstruct from certain painful flashes of memory, is that Candice was affected by watching me return every evening in my cheap Moore's suit and clutching my *Death of a Salesman* sample bag. She started to imagine me in twenty years' time. Receding hairline. Paunch. Not bothering to loosen my tie before heading for the liquor cabinet to pour myself a stiff one. It caused her to have panic attacks. And now I haven't seen Candice for three months.

The Forty Winks Motel has a blinking neon eye on its sign. I am staying here because it is convenient to my work territory, because the weekly rate is cheap, because I will never run into anyone I know, and because the sheer crumminess of my present life will force me to make some decisions. As motel rooms go, this one could be worse. No smell of mould, roach killer, or someone else's semen. The hotplate, provided (illegally) by the motel for an extra four dollars a day, is set up in the bathroom, the only counter space. The bedroom windows don't face the highway out front, but look behind to a new subdivision going up on former farm land. Rows of townhouses disappearing into the vanishing point.

MY FIRST WEEK LIVING HERE, I drove into Toronto, crashing at my friend Aaron's place. Aaron and I go back to high school, but Aaron has a serious girlfriend now, who is eight years older and has a kid, and Aaron let me know in an embarrassed, throat-clearing way that it wasn't really convenient to have me around. I understand that of course, and I'm totally cool about it, so the next Saturday I stayed at Walt's. Walt is single and has never been known to go on a date, but he has three large dogs who were not pleased about having their sofa taken over. Every so often, during the night, I could hear a low growl from behind the kitchen door. All Walt and I ended up doing was watching the ball game while eating Pizza Pizza. Sitting in that dark room, the television flickering and the air heavy with dog flatulence, it occurred to me that all our interesting friends had belonged to Candice.

Which only made me think about how much I missed her.

I will not pretend that it was a mutual break-up. Candice said she didn't love me anymore, and that it had taken her weeks of talking with her therapist and the support of all her friends to get up the courage to leave. She said I was a wonderful person, but she just couldn't be the person she wasn't anymore and she had to save her own life. Tears, nose-blowing. There wasn't much left for me to do but join the chorus of her friends and congratulate her for finding the courage to dump me.

I WAKE UP IN A sweat, a blade of light crossing my face, grope for the dollar-store alarm clock to see why it hasn't rung. Even as I do, I realize it's the weekend. A plunging in my stomach. Oh Jesus, I cannot believe that I feel sickened by the idea of Saturday, that I don't know what I'm going to possibly do with myself.

A grinding outside. I push back the curtain to see a backhoe tearing up the earth in front of the new townhouses. Even though the workers are still finishing the interiors, carrying in sheets of drywall and squares of parquet flooring, the trees and shrubs and grass have arrived in the backs of three dump trucks. Instant neighbourhood.

I reach for my cellphone and start to punch in the code for Candice's number. Then I hit the off button and put the phone down again. Candice is over and I know it. I am not the sort to make useless, grovelling phone calls — besides, I already have. On the other side of the wall, the television goes on and I hear whispers and moans. Somebody is watching a porn flick at seven in the morning. I get up, take a shower, shave and dress, put coffee in the "Little Bachelor" drip machine, open a snack pack of Alpha-Bits. I sit on the edge of the bed crunching letters when I hear "Ode to Joy" reduced to the electronic chimes of my cellphone.

"Mitch, I've finally got you."

"Hey, Mom."

"I've been trying for two days. I was going to call the apartment but you said not to."

"Candice has a lot of stress at work right now. She's really on edge."

"Poor girl. She's too dedicated for her own good."

"Yeah, that's just what I tell her. How's Winnipeg?"

"Mosquitoes already. Marnie Hoffman's aunt got West Nile. She's paralyzed. It's like one of the ten plagues. The rabbi was saying ..."

I take a sip of coffee. My mother did not go to synagogue regularly before my father died. It was Candice, a lapsed Anglican, who encouraged my mother to see it as a way to a new social life. My mother said that if it wasn't for Candice she would have jumped into the grave after my father.

"Are you going to come at the end of June like you said?"

"I said maybe. It really depends on Candice's work. Listen, there's something I've got to do. I'll talk to you later."

"When?"

"Soon."

"You tell that doll not to work so hard."

I really do have something to do. My laundry. When that's finished I stand by my car outside the laundromat, trying not to look at the little kid making faces at me through the window.

Back in the car, I pull onto the highway too quickly, cutting off the driver behind who leans on his horn and gives me the finger. I fiddle with the radio and snap it off again. It is a bright day, perfect early summer weather, but I'm too lethargic to wind down the window. Without thinking I turn into the drive of the Treasure Barn, my tires flinging up stones. The car comes to a halt beside a couple of rain barrels made into begonia planters. Along with the usual rocking chairs outside are white- and black-faced lawn jockeys, several poorly carved wooden ducks, and an old baby carriage full of used videos. There's a sign on the door in wood type that reads OPEN in reverse letters and I wonder if it means the place is actually closed, but the door swings in when I push it.

Through the filter of dust suspended in the air I see dressers from the 1950s, too ugly to be kitsch. A rack of suits in alarming check. Rusting rakes and shovels, imploding sofas, bicycle tire rims, mounted deer antlers. The woman behind the desk — or rather, inside a U-shape made from old jewellery display cases — looks up from her crocheting and smiles. I wonder if that's a real gold tooth she has or just a fake for the weekend tourists. I decide I must buy something, no matter how inferior or useless. And then something catches my eye.

A guitar, and not much of a one — a cheap steel-string with the stencilled image of a bucking bronco on its flat top, which looks as if somebody had started to scrape off the bronco with a pen knife and gave up after removing a hind foot. I pick it up from the broken chair where it lies, put the fraying macramé strap around my neck, and strum a G chord. At least I think it's a G chord. Of course the guitar is out of tune, but the neck looks straight so I take it up to the counter.

"I was wondering how much you want for this," I say.

The woman peers at it over her reading glasses. "That's a Martin. Two hundred."

"It isn't a Martin. It's a *Marvin*. I'll give you twenty-five bucks."

"A hundred."

"Twenty-five."

"I got a case for it. Eighty."

"I'll take the case. Forty."

She sizes me up; a city slicker who thinks he can pull one over on a country bumpkin.

"You got cash?"

I KNOW A FEW CHORDS. Or think I do, because when I get back to the motel room and try to play, I find that my memory isn't too good. Or maybe I don't remember how to tune properly. Whatever the reason, all I get out of that shit-box is a godawful noise. I'm only banging on it for a couple of minutes before the porn addict next door starts pounding his hand on the wall because I'm ruining his appreciation of *New Jersey Housewives*. So I take the guitar and go down the hall and out the back door of the motel. I'd planned to sit at the picnic table but it turns out to be covered in bird shit from seagulls who seem to be lost, so I keep walking, over the collapsing link fence, through tall dandelions gone to feathery seed, to the first lawn of the new subdivision. Nobody seems to be working today and the little bulldozer has been left behind. I walk up the path to the third townhouse, third seems like a good spot, and sit down on the front steps since there's no actual porch. I strum my chords again and then try to pick out a scale, but the truth is I don't know what I'm doing and give up. I stand up again and on a whim try the front door of the townhouse. Lo and behold, it opens.

I've never been inside an unlived-in house before, and it's a strange feeling, both spooky and alluring. This one looks just about finished, the walls painted white, the baseboards and sockets in, the oak-veneer kitchen cupboards installed. The only incongruity is a toilet squatting in the centre of the dining room, like a work by Duchamp. The bannister is still wrapped in plastic. Upstairs, the bedrooms are small but the master bedroom has an ensuite bath. Ah-ha, the bathroom is missing its toilet — thus the one downstairs.

Back on the ground floor, I put down the lid of the toilet and sit. I wonder who will live here and what their story will be. They will eat and laugh and bicker around the kitchen table, watch television in the den, play Monopoly in the basement. The kids will dare each other to enter the dark furnace room, the parents will wait until Saturday night to have sex.

Or maybe such lives don't exist anymore. I know they once did; that's what I fled from in the first place.

ON MONDAY, I USE MY cell to phone Long and McQuade in Toronto. I order an electronic tuner, a set of Martin strings, a capo, a dozen Fender picks, and three instruction books. The bill comes to more than twice what I paid for the guitar.

ON FRIDAY, WHEN I COME in, Fred, the motel owner, looks at me with the placidity of a man who knows that time is an illusion and hands me the package from Long and McQuade. Walking quickly to my room, my sample case in one hand and the package in the other, I fantasize about telling Candice that I have taken up guitar, as if somehow this might impress her the way I had hoped to impress girls when I was twelve. The fantasy is somewhat spoiled by my knowing that Candice would be confirmed in everything she thinks about me, but I'm feeling too expectant to let that get me down. On my bed, I unwrap the goodies and lay them out, everything just so cool. The first thing I do is change the crappy strings. It takes me a good forty-five minutes, puts me in a total sweat, and three times I lance the tip of a finger with the sharp end of a string.

Next, I tune up, checking one of the instruction manuals. *Every Athlete Drinks Gatorade Before Exercising.* Finally, I take one of the fake tortoiseshell picks, smooth and pleasing

to the touch, find my G chord, and strum. To my amazement, the room expands with sweet fullness. Turns out even
a shitbox of a guitar has music sleeping inside it. I strum hard
and faster, but when I get a decent rhythm going, when I'm
starting to feel good and thinking that I could play this one
chord into eternity, the porn addict next door starts pounding on the wall again.

I take the guitar out back, along with the instruction book
and an unrefrigerated beer. I head for the townhouse that I
like to refer to as my own. I am vaguely dismayed by a SOLD
sign on the one next to it, but I march right inside mine, calling, "Honey, I'm home!" and sit on the toilet in the dining
room. With the instruction book open on the floor I practise
these little four-bar exercises. After about ten minutes the
fingertips of my left hand start to get sore, so I skip the next
seven pages of exercises and plunge right into the first song,
"On Top of Old Smoky." Dang, I've always wanted to play
that ol' classic. I make my way haltingly through it, pausing
for a swig of Blue, the working man's beer.

"Candice, babe," I say aloud, "It does not get better than
this."

TODAY I HAVE SEVEN APPOINTMENTS with doctors serving the
suburban Chinese community from shopping mall clinics.
I like these doctors, first or second-generation Canadians
who are less arrogant and dismissive of parasites who feed on
their underbellies. Plus, at lunch time I have my choice of
Chinese restaurants.

Back at the motel, I change into jeans, grab a beer and
my guitar, and head out back towards my townhouse. But,

crossing the street, I hesitate. Someone is at the house on the other side from mine, pounding another SOLD sign into the ground. All I can see is that she is wearing a sweater and a knit skirt too warm for the weather, stockings and heels. I decide to lay the beer down at the roadside and continue on. She is straightening the sign as I come up the walkway. East Indian or Pakistani, pretty but thin, with a beaky nose and a premature streak of silver in her hair.

"Hello there," she says, reaching out. I have to switch the guitar over to take her enthusiastic, real estate agent's handshake. "Beautiful houses, aren't they?"

"Yes, I've been admiring them," I say, not altogether disingenuously. "It looks like they're starting to sell."

"More than half are already gone. The agents are too busy to put up the signs. Everything will be finished in two months. I find it so exciting when a new community begins. It's like instant happiness."

"So, who is moving in?"

"Very nice people, lovely people. Mostly from Mumbai. Originally, I mean."

"Really."

"The builders have some connections there. And there are a lot of Indian people living on the other side of the highway. Maybe you've seen the Hindu temple, it's quite handsome."

"Do you represent this one as well?" I asked, pointing to my house.

"Yes, I do. Would you care to take a look? It has an ensuite master bathroom."

"I know. I mean, I've been inside. The door wasn't locked."

She frowned. "The tradespeople can be so irresponsible. Did you see the basement? Unfinished but very easily done. It would make a good play room for children. Do you have any kids?"

"No. Not yet, anyway."

"It's best to get into the market as early as you can. In housing, prices are always going up. Of course, it is more than an investment. It is your home. Do you know what mortgage you are able to carry?"

"I'm not really sure. I mean, I haven't worked out the fine details."

"What is the down payment you can make?"

I think of the money from my grandfather's estate, which was invested in blue chip funds. I haven't touched it except for taking Candice to Cuba last winter. "I've got about sixty thousand dollars," I say, although actually it's closer to forty.

"That's quite good. Better than most who buy here. With the low interest rates, you would have to pay only nine hundred dollars a month mortgage, plus the tax, heating, and other usual bills. Could you manage that?"

"If I was careful."

"It is good to be careful, I think," she says and smiles. I've never seen a lovelier smile. I'm convinced she really wants me to be happy. "I must tell you that several families have come to see this house in the last two weeks. It won't last long. Here, let me give you my card."

She snaps open her purse, takes out a card, and hands it to me, just as her cellphone starts to ring. I nod to her, but she is already too involved in a conversation about plot surveys to notice, and retreat back across the road, swiping up my beer as I go.

I CONSIDER TELLING EVERY DOCTOR I visit of the various symptoms I have been experiencing lately. Depression punctuated by fleeting moments of desperate exhilaration. On my last call of the day I give in to the need and confess to a family physician whose patients call him "Doctor Dan." Without a word he takes his pad, writes a prescription, and hands it to me.

Rexapro.

"This is one of our competitors' products," I say.

"I think it will suit you better."

"Ours has fewer contra-indications."

"This one is more generally effective, a wider umbrella."

"Really?" I'm disappointed. The vice-president said that ours worked the best for the most people.

"You know what their rep gave me?" Doctor Dan says. "A cappuccino machine. Makes pretty good foam."

BACK AT THE RANCH, I tuck the prescription into the Gideon Bible in the drawer by the bed. I have my usual sumptuous dinner and head out for a night on the town. Along the strip of highway, cars slide past, their lights receding in the dark. It takes me no time to reach Bob's Place, and although it's early in the week, there are a dozen Harley-Davidsons gleaming in the lot. I go up the chipped cement steps and open the door; the music that has been vibrating though the glass windows now blasts me in the face, along with the rank smell of beer. In the dark I can just make out the bikers at their tables, big guys with greying ponytails, leather vests or jackets, beefy hands around their mugs. Also a few women, who match them in bulk and smoke-scarred voices when they laugh. I wonder if they're pissed off about tattoos becoming so popular. The band is crowded into the far corner, thrashing away on some Rush song as if they're playing Maple Leaf Gardens. Most of the bar stools are empty and I pull myself onto one. The bartender, a woman my mother's age (although I doubt my mother would show that amount of cleavage), gives me a friendly smile as she wipes down the bar.

"What can I do you for?"

"I'll have a Blue."

"You got it."

The band takes a break. Only when they come down to join the bikers do I realize they're not young guys. I don't think the bikers are Hells Angels, at least it doesn't say so on their jackets. The beer is so cold it hurts my teeth. Suddenly I have to pee and find the john down the hall from the grease-stinking kitchen. It reeks of piss and marijuana. I relieve myself, decide against touching the sink, and head back to the bar where I down half my beer. My hands are trembling, God knows why, and I slip my right hand into my pocket for some change to jangle but instead my fingers touch the smooth side of a pick. I must have put it in my pocket after practising. I bring out the pick and press it in my palm so that I can feel its rounded corners. I place it on the bar and admire its triangular shape, like it's one of those basic forms of nature.

"You play guitar?" the bartender asks, spotting the pick while she taps a beer.

"Just started really."

"We got an open mic night on Mondays. We could use a fresh face. What's your name?"

She is already taking a clipboard down from a nail beside the shelf holding the hard stuff. I say, "Mitch."

"What's that, a nickname?"

"It's short for Mitchell."

"Okay, Mitch, you're on for next Monday. Eighth slot. We start at seven-thirty. You get a free beer."

"All right," I say.

"You want another?"

"I've got to get up early for work." I take out my wallet and put down a bill and some change. Outside the door, the night air caresses my face, the black star-filled sky sprawls above me. Going down the cement steps I hear grunts, and coming round the building see a couple of bikers beating up some guy, each taking a punch at him in turn, hauling him up for another. I realize that the guy is the lead singer in the band. They let him drop in the dirt and walk past me as they go back into Bob's Place. The singer is up on one knee, spitting blood. I head back down the highway.

ON FRIDAY, THE PRODUCT REPS have a conference at the airport Delta. The star reps are all men in their fifties who never wanted desk jobs. The crowning moment of the day occurs in the conference theatre where a sleek video advertisement showing sunsets and mountain vistas and waterfalls is projected on the huge screen. And then the name *Sopora*, our new sleeping pill. The Canadian vice-president of marketing walks out to a standing ovation, our fists punching the air.

I GET BACK TO THE motel about eight, pulling onto the gravel lot. It isn't as dark as it was a week ago; spring is moving into summer. I drop my crap, throw off my jacket and tie, and pick up the guitar from its case. It was while listening to the vice-president's speech that I suddenly decided what song I wanted to perform at the open mic: Leonard Cohen's "Bird on the Wire." I'd loved the song when I was sixteen — it was so melancholy and cool, and it implied that the singer had experienced a lot of sex and that there would be more in his weary future, but that he would always be moving on. Plus, I still remember the words.

It takes me a full hour to figure out the key and the chord changes. Hearing the A, D, and E chords aren't too hard; it's the B minor that takes me so long, but when I get it the melody falls into place. I can't imagine what it must feel like to create something so yearning, so egotistical, so perfect. I sing and play it over and over, trying to keep in time, make the changes cleaner. When I finally go to bed the tune goes round and round in my head.

SATURDAY MORNING AND I AM standing on the steps of the townhouse, wearing a jacket and tie with my jeans and running shoes. It is a stunning day, the sun bright and buds opening on the spindly trees that have been planted and those still with their roots bundled in burlap. Two blocks down I can see a moving van backed up and two men hefting out a box-spring mattress. The truth is, I wanted to stand here holding a bouquet of flowers, something modest like daisies, but didn't have the nerve. Empty-handed, I watch as Shanti Bhaskar, the real estate agent, pulls up in her Ford

Escort and waves to me as she gets out. To my surprise, she isn't wearing her real estate agent's outfit, but jeans and Converse runners, and she looks really great. "Hi, Mitch," she says, like we're friends, "I'm really glad you called. This whole section is selling out much faster than we anticipated. I know there's another agent in my office showing this one today. Shall we go in?"

"Sure," I say as she comes up. "Of course, I'm not quite ready to decide."

"I understand," she says, touching my arm. "It's a problem. You see something you like, you want to take some time over it, but if you do you'll lose it. You need to accelerate the whole internal process."

Well, I couldn't decelerate any more than I already have. She opens the door and ushers me in. "So," I say, "Any chance you're thinking of buying one around here for yourself?"

"I already bought last year," she laughs. "In the subdivision just south. I wasn't sure that I was ready either but my husband really pushed it. A good thing too, they're already reselling at ten percent higher."

Only now do I see the ring on her hand. Stupidly, I hadn't looked. Inside the house, the toilet is gone from the dining room and the plastic has been removed from the rails. Shanti turns and smiles gently as she looks at me with her brown eyes, as if she knows my disappointment, as if my own skin is as transparent as Saran Wrap.

"I have tried to be free in my way," I say quietly.

"I'm sorry?"

"It's from a Leonard Cohen song."

"Oh, right. 'Bird on the Wire.' Great song."

MONDAY. OPEN MIC TONIGHT. I pull into my gravel spot, throw myself out of the car, fumble with the key to open the motel room, yank the guitar out of its case, and start to practise. I fuck up totally. Calm down, calm down. I put the guitar onto the spongy armchair, take off my suit, and step into the shower. I decide not to shave again and dress in jeans, untucked lumberjack shirt, sneakers. I heat up a can of Campbell's chunky beef soup and, taking the pot, perch on the bed and look out the window to the townhouses across the way. The streetlights are working now, casting overlapping circles on the street and the little front lawns. I eat a few spoonfuls before putting down the pot and taking up the guitar again. And now the time is already gone and I put the guitar in its case, wondering why I don't chicken out. But I go out the door and walk along the highway holding my guitar case, like the figure on the cover of some pathetic folk record.

The parking lot of Bob's Place has half the usual number of motorcycles parked out front, Monday not being the most popular night of the week. Inside, I have to let my eyes adjust to see three young guys already setting up their Fenders and a small drum kit. I make my way to the bar where the bartender is filling ketchup bottles.

"Hey there," she says. "Number eight on the list, right?"

"I think so."

"You want a Blue?"

"Thanks."

"I remember what everybody drinks. It's just a memory thing I have. Even if you don't come in for three months, I remember. Not that it's going to do me any good, with the place shutting down."

"What do you mean?"

She slides the beer in front of me, a line of foam slipping down the cold glass. "Going to be a Valu-Mart here. Groceries and shit. For the new subdivision. And a half-mile down the road there's going to be a mall with six movie screens. Hey!" she shouts to the band. "Why don't you stop messing around with the damn mics and start playing?"

But the band takes another few minutes. The lead singer does this weird snake motion while he sings and then their three songs are over and two women in suede vests are already coming up. One has a regular guitar, the other a Dobro, and they sing two Loretta Lynn songs and sound all right, like they've been playing in crummy Nashville honky-tonks for years. Louder applause from the bikers. The bartender slides over to me.

"You're on next, honey."

"But I'm number eight."

"Well, number three has pussied out and number four is in the washroom so I'm slipping you in. You go and rock this place, tiger."

It takes a total refutation of all my instincts to get myself to pick up the guitar case and carry it across the room. It knocks against the arm of a biker who shoves me back hard. By the time I reach the stage I am shaking like a man pulled out of an icy river. I pull the macramé strap over my head, take the pick from my pocket, and perch on the stool. The glare from the small spotlight turns the audience dark and menacing, which they actually are.

"Get the fuck on with it."

MY CELLPHONE IS CHIMING on the night table by the motel bed as I unlock the door. I take my time putting down my case, dropping the keys, walking over to pick up the phone. The numbers pulsing on the little screen are Candice's. I stare at them as if I'm looking at the winning numbers of a lottery ticket that I've already thrown away.

"Hello?" I say tentatively.

"Mitch. I've been phoning all night." I can hear the shakiness in her voice but also the annoyance. "I need to talk to you. Come over."

"It's midnight. I'm a forty-five minute drive away."

"It's kind of important, Mitch."

"It's over then, the new thing?"

"I was an idiot. No, not an idiot. I mean I understand myself better now, what I had to put myself through."

"Us. Put us through."

"Yes, us. I need you, Mitch."

"I just played a song," I say.

"What?"

"In a bar. A biker bar, if you can believe it. I got up with a guitar and sang 'Bird on the Wire.' When I got down again the bartender, this older woman, she had tears in her eyes. She said to me, 'Bob used to sing me that song.'"

"Mitch, I don't know what you're talking about."

A TULIP BULB LOOKS LIKE a little onion, like you could bite into it. I put one into each of the small holes I've dug with a spoon and pat down the earth. It's too late for them to bloom this year, but they'll come up next spring.

On the next lawn two young boys are tussling over a soccer ball. Their names are Daya and Rajif. Some older kids have made a ramp out of a sheet of plywood and some blocks left by the construction company and are taking turns jumping on their skateboards. It is an absolutely beautiful morning, like the sun has risen for the first time over the world.

I hear my name and look up to see Mrs. Kankipati crossing the street with a plate in her hands. She is a handsome woman with greying hair and large brown eyes whose husband is an importer who flies to Kashmir every six weeks. Mrs. Kankipati says, "Mitch, I just made some pakoras. I think you will like them."

"Oh, I love pakoras."

"But in the restaurant it isn't the same. You try one of these."

She holds up the plate and I take one. It is almost too hot to hold and leaves oil on my fingers. It is savoury and delicious.

"Amazing, Mrs. K."

"You need a wife to cook for you. Maybe a nice Indian girl, what do you think?"

"I need to learn how to cook. Then I'll bring you over something."

We both laugh and she puts the plate down on the grass and retreats back to her own house. I return to my gardening, knees pressing into the still-new grass, the smell of the earth in my nostrils. The cries of seagulls and the steady hum of traffic from the highway remind me of the ocean.

# I Find I Am Not Alone on the Island

IN THE SUMMER OF 1989, Chloe Tillman was working in a diner while dithering about going to graduate school. She had been accepted at Princeton and offered a scholarship, but had so far failed to convince herself that the intense study of difficult texts was a worthwhile or even defensible pursuit. It was one of those rare periods when she was without a boyfriend, having dumped Tim Veldhuisen in April. Tim had started to say "I love you" and give hints that he was working up the nerve to ask her to move in with him. The thought of waking up every day beside him had filled her with dread. The truth was she hadn't been in love with any of her boyfriends, a nagging secret that she had kept from even her closest girlfriends. She did miss Tim for a couple of weeks, but she took the measure of her happiness and decided that she had made the right decision.

The diner was at Yonge and Wellesley, before that part of town had begun to change. The customers were tourists walking down to the Eaton Centre, strippers on their way to work in the nearby clubs, provincial government office workers, and those who Liana, the owner's daughter, lumped under the category of "freaks." Chloe always gave large portions to the strippers, who called her "dear" or "honey." Her favourite customer, a pleasant, balding man with round black glasses who always left a twenty percent tip or better, liked to sit under the framed print of the Parthenon by the kitchen door. He was friendly without trying to flirt, and he was funny but didn't try to make her linger at his table. His order was a western sandwich, a Greek salad, or occasionally a tuna melt, which he blamed for his "middle-aged swell." Every so often he would joke about his daughter, his son, or his wife, but always in an affectionate way (she despised male customers who made cracks about their wives). He claimed that one day he would quit his government job, buy a sailboat, and take them all to the Caribbean — this despite his never having gone sailing in his life and being, he said, afraid of large bodies of water. He'd been working for the province for seventeen years but claimed not to know what his actual responsibilities were other than to furrow his brow and tap his pencil on those rare occasions when the minister came in.

He always carried a book and read over lunch — one of the classics of western literature: *Madame Bovary*, *Crime and Punishment*, *Middlemarch*. She asked him about his reading and he told her that he'd only developed a taste for fiction in the last few years and was now trying to catch up. "But I'm hoping to die of old age before I get to James Joyce." He'd heard a little about her, too — where she came from, what she studied, her dilemma over graduate school. "Well, I'm impressed by Princeton. If I were you, I'd go just to make other people feel stupid. I mean, you're making me feel stupid right now and you haven't even accepted."

And then he stopped coming. He had occasionally missed a day, and so it was half a week before she registered his absence and another couple of days before she began to really wonder. Perhaps he was on vacation with his wife and kids, or was sick. Perhaps he'd dropped dead or been hit by a car, although she didn't consider those possibilities. She was disappointed to think that he was taking his meals elsewhere.

The last time Chloe saw him he'd been reading *Robinson Crusoe*. While she wiped down the table next to his, he told her what a great adventure story it was. "I feel like I'm twelve years old again." He joked that he might try to survive on an island using the book as a guide and she reminded him that he was going to buy that sailboat. "You're right," he had said. "I almost forgot. There's this really great line in the book. I underlined it, which is a bit nerdy of me, I know. Want to see?"

He'd held the book up and she had read the underlined words. *I find I am not alone on the island*. She had agreed that it was a great line although privately she had thought it a little awkward and then she had gone into the kitchen. When she came out again, he was gone, leaving some bills and change on the table.

Picking up a lunch order, she said to Liana, "Have you seen that middle-aged guy with the black glasses lately? The one who always sits at number seven?"

"I need a little more information here. How does he take his coffee?"

"Cream, not milk. Sometimes he orders the apple pie."

"Oh sure. Good tipper. But you usually serve him. I can't really picture his face."

"He hasn't been in for a couple of weeks."

"He hit on you or something?"

"No, he's not creepy. I was just wondering."

"You ever notice how you can tell people are on blind dates? The way they say the person's name as if it's a question. *Melanie? Simon?* I always want to say, 'Go home, both of you, before it's too late.'"

IN THE NEXT WEEK, TIM left two messages on her answering machine. She started running in the early evenings. Her friend Natalie called from Paris, where she had gone to study art history. She didn't know anybody yet and was lonely; why didn't Chloe come and stay with her for a week or ten days at the end of August? She might be able to pick up a cheap last-minute ticket. But Chloe dithered on that, too.

And then on Friday she was setting a table when she saw the man's photograph, a small black-and-white shot on the front page of some government newsletter left on a chair. The photograph looked five or ten years old; the man still had all his hair.

*Economics Development Officer Fondly Remembered.*

So, she thought, he really was dead after all. His name was Gerry Lembeck. He had been a "vital" part of the negotiating team that had kept two automotive plants in Ontario. He had died "suddenly" — that was all it said, except that for years he had bravely struggled with an unspecified illness. He left behind his wife, Rita, head of personnel for a chain of pharmacies, his son Joe and two-year-old daughter Naomi. A memorial had already been held for ministry employees.

She showed the article to Liana. "You know what 'suddenly' means, don't you?" Liana said. "It's code for suicide. I'm guessing the illness was depression. Did he seem depressed to you?"

"No," Chloe said. "I mean, yes. Maybe. I don't know."

She meant to take the article but somehow it wasn't in her bag when she got home. At ten o'clock her friends came to get her and they cabbed it to a club on King Street to see a band called the Stuffed Triggers. In the crowd they met up with more friends, including a guy named Daniel, a theatre major at George Brown. She had a rule against going out with actors, since in her experience they were all revoltingly needy narcissists, but Daniel was funny and good-looking and tall (which always attracted her), and he never once talked about his acting ambitions. In the early morning hours he walked her all the way home, telling her about his family's disappointment that he didn't want to go into the building trades. He made her laugh, so she took him upstairs. He was quite beautiful in the pre-dawn dark, his sleek back, his chest, his face. It didn't feel like a first time. Afterwards, she easily fell asleep.

HER PARENTS LIVED IN A hundred-and-twenty-year-old farm house in Newmarket. The lawn sloped down to the river where her father kept his canoe and rowboat. Some of the surrounding land was being developed into suburban housing but in back of the house, with the surrounding spruce trees and the willows by the water, it was possible for her to have the illusion that little had changed since her childhood. Her father was a retired high school science teacher; her mother had taught physical education and home economics. Their house, with its mismatched farm-sale furniture, worn rugs, and books, had long ago set her own tastes. Every friend she had ever brought here had immediately fallen in love with both the house and her parents, and when her father would start handing out the martinis at four o'clock, the friend would invariably ask to be adopted. What her friends saw, Chloe always thought, was no more or less valid than how any other household presented itself.

She found her father reading *Scientific American* in a Muskoka chair, their golden lab at his feet. Her mother, in rubber knee pads, was weeding the garden. She and her father hugged lightly while her mother took off her gloves, saying she was glad for an excuse to stop. Her father asked whether she had decided yet about Princeton, giving her his "patented" look, meaning that he couldn't imagine what was holding her up. Her mother changed the subject to Chloe's sisters — to May, who had given up trying to get pregnant and was hoping to adopt a baby from China, and to Lauren, who had just started to date a year after her divorce.

They asked her about Tim, who she had made the mistake of bringing up to visit and who had made almost too good an impression. She said nothing about Daniel, of whom they were less likely to approve. After an hour or so she grew restless and announced an intention to take out the canoe. "You won't enjoy it," her father said. "You can see all those new houses along the way. And now there's always trash floating in the river."

She went anyway, the dog wagging anxiously from the shore as she pushed out. Her father was right about the garbage: she saw a floating Coke can, a broken chair, plastic bags snagged on the willow branches. She was an elegant canoeist and her strokes were almost silent. It didn't surprise her when she started to cry, for she had felt it building for a couple of days. She drifted until she grew quiet again and then she turned around. By the time she reached her parents' house, she had recovered.

ON MONDAY MORNING, SHE RODE her old Schwinn bike to work in the rain. Liana put an Aretha Franklin tape on the stereo and made Chloe laugh by lip-syncing as she carried platters of eggs and home fries. The rain came down harder, pounding on the plate glass windows. All day, people threw themselves in through the doorway, hanging up their dripping coats. Cleaning up her last table, Chloe found an umbrella hooked to the back of a chair.

"We scored a Gucci," she said to Liana. "Unless it's a fake."

"There must be four in the box already. Take your pick."

"I can't see holding up an umbrella while I'm riding."

She went into the back storage room and pulled the lost-and-found box from under the counter. Amidst the single gloves and key chains and empty wallets she saw a Penguin edition of *Robinson Crusoe*. She reached in and picked it up, holding it close to her face. Carefully she turned the cover and saw the initials *GL* written on the corner of the first page.

OF COURSE IT WAS HER duty to return the book to Gerry Lembeck's family. It might only be a paperback, but it was one of his last possessions and might mean something to his wife or his children. In the white pages she found a listing for a G. Lembeck on Ava Road. She picked up the telephone receiver and hesitated. Perhaps it was the wrong moment, coming so soon after the funeral. She could mail it, but wouldn't that look weird? No, she would have to phone. She started to dial when a knock sounded on the door.

"Who is it?"

"Daniel. I've brought take-out Chinese and beer."

She smiled and, putting down the receiver, hurried to let him in.

SHE SAW DANIEL EVERY DAY for rest of the summer. They slipped easily into one another's lives, spending the night either at her place on Clinton or his on Baldwin. They went to old films at the Bloor, browsed in used bookshops on Harbord. One weekend they took the bus to a music festival in Guelph. She cared for him more than she had for anyone before, but was it enough, what she felt?

Not enough, in the end, to keep her from going to New Jersey.

AT PRINCETON, SHE HAD A miserable affair with a professor, failed to end it several times and worried that it was the guilt and terror rather than love that held her. Deciding that she had to get away, she applied to the Ph.D. program at Berkeley.

What healed her was the beauty of northern California and an increasing passion for her work. For a time, that was enough; but in her second year she had two relationships in quick succession and then a third, all with fellow students and none of lasting significance. In her final two years, while writing her thesis, she became involved with an instructor on contract named Amjad Far. He was handsome and very sharp and with a solemn temperament that made her feel very safe, and, feeling that she might start to love him, she agreed to move in. She defended her thesis, and as she began to apply for jobs Amjad returned to Iran for two months. A tenure track position at the University of Toronto came up and she flew in to give a guest lecture. Amjad returned, but having a new beard wasn't all that had changed about him. His eyes would turn hard if she spoke to another man at a party. He insisted that they both abstain from drinking. One day he grew angry over the skirt she wore, the first time he had ever raised his voice. She developed insomnia and became so thin that her former thesis advisor drew her aside and suggested that she seek help at the eating disorder clinic. What she finally did made her feel ashamed for its cowardliness: winning the job in Toronto, she waited until Amjad left for a weekend retreat with some friends, packed up her things, and took a taxi to the airport.

HER MOTHER UNDERWENT HIP REPLACEMENT surgery and afterwards her father began to talk about moving to a place that was easier to look after. Her older sister had split from her husband and the two were in a custody fight over their adopted daughter. Her other sister, the most wild of the three, had quit her job to become a fitness instructor.

Chloe reworked her thesis, which was accepted by Duke University Press, and began a new manuscript. At thirty-two she had a few fine lines around her mouth, the first strands of silver in her hair, but her friends said that she was only growing more beautiful. She remained determinedly single, glad for the silence of the small house she had found on Major Street. In the afternoon she heard children coming home from school. Her days were full with teaching, research, new administrative duties, and more than her share of graduate students to advise.

She met Lester at a small dinner party given by her department head. A friend of the host, he was a sous-chef at the Sutton Place Hotel and had offered to cook. Perhaps there was something irresistibly romantic about watching a young chef (he wasn't yet thirty) hurrying from the kitchen, telling everyone to eat while the food was hot, laughing as he swept up his own glass of wine before heading back. Finally he sat down next to her. At the end of the evening, she was trying to work up the nerve to ask for his phone number when he asked for hers.

He was half Jewish and half Irish-Catholic, one of six children. Six months later she knew that she loved him with a certainty that was no more explainable than the doubt in all her previous relationships, and she asked him to move into her house. Their first daughter was born in the spring of 2001, and their son two years after that. She took year-long maternity leaves and afterwards they shared parenting duties.

Work on the second book slowed to a crawl and did not pick up again until the fall that her younger one started daycare. A new semester was beginning and it was her turn to teach the dreaded introductory course. She had to lecture from a stage with a microphone, but her first-class jitters were not as pronounced as they had once been and before long she was hardly glancing at her notes. It was only after she had met with the teaching assistants and was packing up her satchel that she had a chance to scan the names on the class list. Halfway down the second column, she saw: *Lembeck, Naomi.*

Her heart began to race even before she understood what the name might mean to her. She gathered her notes, walked to her bike, which was chained in front of Victoria College, and rode home. Inside, she dumped her things and hurried up to the study. The attic ran the length of the house and the walls were lined with double-rows of books, but although she hadn't seen it in years and couldn't even remember bringing it with her from Toronto to Princeton to Berkeley and back to Toronto again, she went to the back wall, leaned down to the bottom corner shelf, pulled out the books in front, and found the *Robinson Crusoe.*

SHE FOUND IT STRANGE THAT she even remembered his name, and that she was so certain this particular Naomi Lembeck was the daughter of the man she had briefly known. She brought the book to her lectures and kept it with her during office hours. She rehearsed the scene in her mind, how Naomi would come up to her at the lectern or knock at the office door, asking about the last lecture or the next essay, and how she would ask her to sit down and then in the briefest manner possible tell her about this small connection to her father. Then she would reach into her satchel and draw out the book, handing it over without ceremony. Of course it might not go as she hoped; instead of astonishment and tears, the young woman might become angry or resentful. But she was willing to suffer what came.

Although she didn't know what Naomi Lembeck looked like, and could not really remember the father either, she would sometimes scan the rising tiers of seats looking for some glint of recognition — the shape of a mouth, something in the eyes. Then, during a lecture a third of the way into the semester and when Chloe was starting to consider sending Naomi a note via email, a woman got up and left the lecture hall. Not unobtrusively but noisily, fumbling her things, pushing her way past the row of knees, stumbling on the stairs. Chloe glimpsed only the side of her face, the dark hair, and then when she was on the stairs, the heavyset body in shiny jacket and jeans and boots, but she knew, she just knew. She had to stop herself from running up the stairs after the woman. But after the lecture she thought: my imagination is overheating itself.

The following Monday, she received by university mail a revised student list. Naomi Lembeck was one of three students who had withdrawn from the course.

CHLOE SENT HER AN EMAIL, simply asking that Ms. Lembeck come and see her. When after a week she had still not received a response, she sent another, only to have it bounce back as undeliverable. She checked with the admissions office and was told that the woman had dropped out of school.

She could have persisted, asking the admissions office for a telephone number, Googling her name or joining Facebook. She had this sickening feeling that she had failed Gerry Lembeck, that the reason she had met him all those years ago was so that she might now reach out to his daughter. But of course she knew this was nonsense, a delusion to place oneself at the centre of every story. Chasing Naomi Lembeck would have been excessive and even weird. Who was to say that *this* Naomi Lembeck really was the daughter of Gerry?

She did, however, continue to carry the book in her satchel until the end of the semester, after which it was returned to the low corner shelf, back row.

THEY WERE HAVING DINNER ONE evening in early April — Lester cooking for her and the girls and their neighbours, Allan and Lynn and their two boys, along with the teenage sitter, Odile, who picked the kids up from school and was having a bad day because of an argument with her boyfriend. Apropos of nothing, she thought of Gerry Lembeck's daughter. She couldn't remember her name at the moment but that same sickening feeling came back to her. She had to make herself breathe evenly.

She said aloud, "I find I am not alone on the island."

Nathalie, their girl, said, "Are we going to an island?"

Lester said, "It sounds like one of your mom's literary quotations."

"Are we supposed to guess where it's from?" Odile said. "It sounds like poetry."

"I haven't read a poem since the end of high school," Allan said. "That one by T.S. Eliot. With the ragged claws. I was nuts about that poem."

"I used to know this man a long time ago," Chloe said. "He showed me that line in a book. Gerry Lembeck."

"That's a funny name," said Jack, their son. "Lem*peck?* Lem*puck?*"

"Who was he?" Lester said.

"I don't really know that much about him. He liked cream in his coffee. He must be dead sixteen or seventeen years now."

"Mommy, do we have to talk about dead people?"

"Doesn't the food look delicious?" Lynn said. "Lester, you spoil us all. How are the kids ever going to go to McDonald's with their friends?"

"I like McDonald's better," Lynn's older boy, Danny, said.

"Ouch," said Lester, putting his hands to his heart. He leaned towards Chloe and said into her ear, "Are you okay?"

"Sure." And then more loudly, "What are we all waiting for? Let's eat."

"I'm already eating," Natalie said with her mouth full.

Chloe made a face at her, picked up her own fork, and took a bite. "It's heaven," she said.

# Wolf

HE COULDN'T SLEEP ON THE plane, despite the eye-mask, the earplugs, the pill. He only managed another ten pages of the Heinrich Böll novel before he gave in and watched not one but two Adam Sandler movies on the overhead screen. At seventy-seven it wasn't so easy travelling — this was his last thought before finally falling asleep, only to be awakened as the plane thumped onto the runway at Frankfurt. Then he had to gather his things and rush to make his connecting flight. Landing again at Tegel Airport, he felt as if he couldn't add three numbers together. But nobody asked him anything, not even the slight German customs agent in the unthreatening green uniform, like a postal clerk, who merely stamped his passport and wished him a pleasant stay. The luggage arrived on the sleek conveyer and an educated-sounding German in a cardigan loaded it into his spotless cab.

Anywhere else, Bernie would have chatted with the driver

about his family, his native land (at home they were always immigrants), but here he didn't know how to begin. *I'm Bernie Feinberg, a Jew from Toronto who's here to visit his grand-daughter. She's writing a thesis on Heinrich Böll who, between you and me, I'd never heard of before.* The driver gave him a smooth ride to the front of the Sofitel in the Gendarmenmarkt. Even in his exhaustion he took in the lovely square, how a woman crossed the cobblestones in long strides, one hand holding closed her long coat. The October sky was the colour of aluminum.

In the hotel room, he saw the red light blinking on the telephone: instructions from Sarah on how to get to a Turkish restaurant for dinner. She hadn't sounded all that enthusiastic when he phoned to tell her of his visit, and he was relieved to hear her recorded voice, as if there had been the possibility that he might not be able to find her. She was the first grandchild. They had been close when she was little, he and Ida taking her for afternoons and later whole week-ends. But when she got a little older she preferred overnights with her friends, and then came the harrowing teenage years, the details of which they had been denied. She had turned into a poised and beautiful adult, but the closeness had never returned. If Ida were alive, maybe things would be different, but what could he, a retired box manufacturer, have to say that would be interesting to a university student who was "into" philosophy, literature, politics, and who knew what else? Still, she was his granddaughter, his oldest boy's first child, and surely he had a duty to come and see her.

He unpacked his suitcase, putting his pressed shirts, ties, underwear, and socks in the drawers and hanging up his clean suit. He took a shower in the gleaming bathroom and lay down on the bed where he immediately fell asleep.

Stirring awake, he was sure that Ida lay under the blanket next to him; he even reached out to touch her broad back, before she vanished. He forced himself up, shaved in the bathroom, telephoned the front desk to ask for someone to pick up the suit he had travelled in, dressed, and went out.

His hotel was in Mitte, the neighbourhood that had once again become the centre of Berlin. He spent the afternoon within its invisible boundaries, walking the broad Unter den Linden, looking up at the cobalt-blue mosaics of the Ishtar Gate in the Pergamon Museum. He visited two smaller memorials: the red sandstone sculpture on Rosenstrasse and the empty shelves beneath a square of glass in the ground in Bebelplatz. Then he set out for the new Holocaust memorial south of the Brandenburg Gate, a field of rectangular concrete blocks standing on undulating ground. A maze, a work of sculpture, a make-believe cemetery, a playground for the children clambering over the blocks. This was somehow supposed to show how sorry they were?

He imagined what he might say to Sarah: *I didn't feel qualified to judge it.* He felt as if all his responses were caught in a little glass bowl somewhere to the right of his heart. He went into a newsstand for a paper, but could find only an English magazine called *ExBerliner*, which he took to a café, sat at a little table by the window, and ordered a coffee. Perhaps she hadn't sufficiently prepared himself for the trip, although he wasn't sure what he ought to have done. The first article he read was a profile of a woman, a well-known Berlin journalist in her sixties, who had just published a memoir that tried to come to terms with her father having been in the SS. When she had been ten years old, the article said, her father had stood up in church, denounced modern Germany, called out a farewell to his fellow officers, and shot himself in the head.

He closed the magazine and looked up. Two well-dressed young children were eating ice cream cones. Their parents, standing behind them, were engaged in earnest conversation. One of the children, the girl, saw him staring. She waved to him solemnly.

THE RESTAURANT SARAH HAD chosen had carpets on the walls, shelves lined with bowls, vases of beaten copper. Middle Eastern music played softly. She was already at a table, reading a book. Her hair was tied back, she wore no makeup, and her face looked too thin. A striped scarf was wound around her neck. She looked up and smiled, closing the book as she rose, her face inscrutable to him, secretive. He walked towards the table and as they hugged he kissed her ear.

"Zeyde, you're actually here."

"I can't quite believe it myself. I was never the sort to just pick up and get on a plane. But then of course I had to run the business ..."

He let the sentence die out, for he didn't want to talk in his usual way, boring the young people. He started again: "I had a very interesting afternoon. I saw the new memorial."

"Do you want to look at the menu?" Perhaps she hadn't heard him. "Thank goodness for Turkish restaurants. If it wasn't for them I'd have to eat that heavy German food all the time. We can share some dishes, unless you'd rather order your own."

"I put myself in your hands."

The waiter arrived and Sarah ordered in German, hesitant but nevertheless impressive. Listening to the waiter answer, he realized that he had been hearing the language spoken all afternoon and that it had sounded not harsh or aggressive but pleasing to the ear. He had once been able to speak a simple Yiddish, but now, with his parents gone almost twenty years, he'd forgotten most of it.

"Do you want a beer?" Sarah said. "German beer really is spectacular."

"Yes, I would," he said, although he rarely drank. Nowadays young Jewish people seemed to like their liquor as much as everyone else. Over dinner, he gave a report of the family back home. She told him of difficulties getting a telephone and internet service, here where one expected such services to be quickly and efficiently provided. Mostly she talked about her work, how being in Berlin had changed her perspective; writing about Germany before, she said, had been like trying to describe a wolf without having actually seen one.

Why a wolf? he thought, eating from the delicious little mounds of food and sipping tentatively at the beer. He was thinking about having something sweet when Sarah said, "What time is it? I promised to meet a friend. I hope that's all right, Zeyde. There's a lecture we're supposed to go to."

He decided not to ask about the "we." "Of course. Don't

worry, I'll make my way back to the hotel. We can get to-gether tomorrow."

"I'm not so sure about tomorrow. I have a lot to do."

"Even an hour would be nice. I'm only here for a few days."

"Sure. How about coffee in the afternoon? We can meet at my favourite café in Kreutzberg. I'll write down the corner. Say three o'clock?"

"Any time is good. I'm not on a schedule."

ON ANY OF HIS TRIPS with Ida they would have taken a cab home, but the U-Bahn station was right at the corner. He walked onto the platform without passing any barriers and stood in front of the automatic ticket machine, trying to figure out what to punch when a woman in an imitation fur stepped up. There was no need to give the ticket to anyone or get it stamped, she said, but only to hold onto it in case an inspector, disguised as a businessman or a hippy, came through the train. He had to take the U7 line, changing to the U6 and getting off at Stadtmitte. The train he got into was modern and well-lit and he enjoyed the ride until two young men in studded leather jackets and black boots came into the car, each with a Dobermann pinscher on a chain. Were they neo-Nazis or some other sort of danger-ous type? Would they notice the little Israeli pin in the lapel of his coat that he'd received for a charitable donation and never wore at home but had put on just before leaving for the airport? But they ignored him, and when his stop came he stood quickly up, pressed the illuminated button by the doors, and got off.

His heart beat fast as he walked to the hotel. Although he felt exhausted, he propped himself up in bed and tried to read *The Clown*. He managed two-and-a-half pages before putting it down and turning out the light. But the time-change kept him awake for a long time.

AT A NEWSSTAND IN HACKESCHER Markt he bought five post-card scenes of Berlin at the end of the war: buildings turned to rubble, smoke and flames rising. He couldn't imagine how people could live with such images of their past on constant display.

He began to walk, his guidebook concealed in the pocket of his cloth overcoat so that he would not look like a tourist. The Germans were a well-dressed people, but then they had grown rich after the war, with the help of America. He would have liked to start a conversation with an actual Berliner, but he had never been the sort of person who could speak to strangers, not like Ida.

He strolled along the River Spree, wide and pleasant, then turned into the small streets. He passed a marionette theatre, several German restaurants, an internet café. He came to a window with a few old carving tools displayed behind it and, peering through the doorway, saw a man in a leather apron working at a bench. On the wall hung violins, their varnish gleaming. A few were unfinished, the bare wood almost white. He'd never paid music the slightest attention but so charmed was he by the sight that he stepped inside.

The man said something in German without looking up and went on with his work, using a small gouging tool to shape the scroll on the end of a neck. Bernie saw piles of roughly cut tops and backs, smelled wood dust and varnish. The gouge hissed softly.

The man in the apron straightened up. He had a large, peanut-shaped face. There was sawdust stuck to his glasses.

"Do you speak English? You do beautiful work."

"Thank you."

"My grandson plays violin."

"Ah, so."

"Are they very expensive?"

"Not so, I think."

The man turned and lifted one of his violins off the wall. He held it out for Bernie to take. It was surprisingly light, an egg shell, and looked both new and antique at the same time. He wondered how a person even judged a violin.

"This is very good wood. Spruce from Bosnia. The rest, maple from Switzerland. I polish it for many hours. No one else is doing this but me."

"You mean that you are the only builder in Berlin?"

"No, no, there are others. I mean, no one else touches this one."

"I see. How much is it?"

"Three thousand, five hundred Euros. With case and bow."

In dollars that was perhaps five thousand. Of course he had no intention of actually buying it, but he continued to stand there with the instrument in his hand.

"I can sell for maybe a hundred Euros less."

He told himself to give it back to the builder, but it remained in his hands.

WALKING THROUGH THE STREETS OF Kreutzberg, he held tightly onto the handle of the violin case. Perhaps he would be mistaken for a musician, on his way to have a little coffee before a rehearsal at the Philharmonic. He felt giddy for having spent so much money so impulsively; foolish, certainly, but also triumphant. Music, after all, was the best thing that the Germans had given the world. Who knew, maybe the violin would change his grandson's life. An impulsive gesture could do that.

He fished in his pocket for the address that Sarah had given him, and when he couldn't find it, his heart had a panicky flutter. But no, there it was, lodged between the pages of the guidebook. He looked at the map, found that he was only a block away, hurried now, caught sight of the awning, the small wooden tables and café chairs stacked up. Inside it was crowded and humming with voices, clouded with cigarette smoke. There were music posters on the walls, and handbills at the counter. Nobody in the place looked older than twenty-five. He saw Sarah and moved between the tables towards her, holding up the violin case so as not to smack anyone with it. Only as he got closer did he see that she was sitting with a young man. Wire glasses, a loose sweater of indeterminate colour, with a scarf around his neck. They were speaking quietly. Sarah did not see him until he was by the table.

"Zeyde," she said, getting up to hug him, more warmly than on their first encounter, although he wondered whether she was doing it for the benefit of the young man.

"I was worried that you would get lost. This is my friend Paul."

The young man had risen and now took Bernie's hand. "I am glad to meet you. I hope you don't mind my coming."

"Of course not. I like young people." What a stupid thing to say. Was he a friend of Sarah's or a boyfriend?

He had some trouble manoeuvring the case under the table. Sarah said, "Is that a violin?"

"I bought it this afternoon. It's for Brent."

"You bought a violin for Brent?"

"Don't you know that he's taking lessons?"

"May we see it?" Paul asked.

"Sure. Do you play?"

"In school I played the cello. My uncle is quite a good violinist. He plays in a string quartet in Potsdam."

Bernie had brought the case up and laid it on his lap. He undid the latches and opened the top. Paul whistled softly. "It's very beautiful," he said.

"Zeyde, Brent is *seven* years old. Aunt Maureen is forcing him to take lessons. He wants to play hockey. And it's full size — it's too big for him."

Bernie shut the case and closed the latches. "He'll grow into it," he said gruffly, pushing the case back under the table. The waiter came and he immediately ordered a tea. Sarah and Paul ordered beers. He said to Paul, "Were you born in Berlin?"

"No, in the country, a small village."

"And both your parents were German?"

"Yes."

"And your grandparents? They were here, in the thirties, the forties?"

He hadn't meant to sound quite so aggressive; perhaps he

was annoyed at Sarah for her skepticism about the violin. Paul said, "Perhaps you are asking if they were in the war. My maternal grandfather was in the navy. He helped to sink two British ships. My paternal grandfather was in the infantry. He was shot by a Russian soldier and lost his leg."

"Is that what you're asking, Zeyde?"

"The service is very slow here," Bernie said.

Their drinks came. Sarah looked angry, although he'd hardly done anything wrong. He could hear Ida's sighing voice: *Well, are you happy with your performance this evening? Do you think it makes you look clever?* The only one who didn't seem out of sorts was Paul, who asked Bernie about what he had seen and done in Berlin. He felt a sudden gratitude to the young man.

"Such a nice violin," Paul said, as Bernie was counting out money for the bill. "Maybe you will learn to play it."

"It's a little late for that," Bernie said. "Arthritis. Besides, I don't know a thing about music. I never had the ear for it."

They got up. Sarah said, almost reluctantly, "What are you doing tomorrow?"

"I'm going to that concentration camp north of Berlin."

Paul said, "I don't think Jews should visit the camps. I think only Germans should go."

"Zeyde, maybe it's not a good idea."

"I was almost fifteen years old when I first heard about them. We saw pictures in the newspapers."

"I offer to go with you," Paul said.

"Paul, stop it."

"Stop what? If your grandfather wants to go to Sachsenhausen, perhaps it's better I go with him. It's confusing to get there. Very tiring by the time you leave. I will come, Bernie."

"That is very kind of you."

"Well, I'm definitely not doing this," Sarah said.

"I didn't mean to cause an argument."

"There is no argument. What time shall I come to the hotel?"

"Nine o'clock suits me."

"Okay, good."

Outside, they stood in the light cast by the café. Bernie took a breath, wondering what to say to ease the grim expression on Sarah's face. But all he managed was "It isn't polluted, not like Paris. There isn't nearly as much traffic."

They walked him to the U-Bahn. On the train, he wasn't sitting long, the violin in his lap, before his eyes began to close. He snored, woke himself, and blinked at the other passengers, who were not the same as when he had closed his eyes. The train was just pulling out of a station whose name he did not recognize. He must have passed his stop. He stood up, his legs feeling weak, and, clutching the violin case, waited by the doors. It took several minutes to arrive at the next station, where he impatiently pushed the button for the doors to open.

The platform was deserted; even the sandwich kiosk was closed. He walked to the iron stairs and climbed to the entrance, but there were no officials here either. He felt his confidence seep away and didn't trust himself to get back on a train and return the way he had come. Instead, he would look for a taxi. Here the night was gloomy, the station surrounded by trees in full leaf and, more distant, office buildings. A few cars went by, but no taxis. He was trying to decide whether he had any choice but to risk the U-bahn again when something smacked him hard from behind, propelling the violin case from his hands as he fell forward. Sharp pains stabbed his hands and knees and he could only stay where he was, trying to catch his breath.

People leaned towards him, their faces close, speaking German.

"I'm all right. I can get up now."

"English?" a woman said. She took his arm as he rose. "Teenage girls. They are now as bad as the boys. They stole your violin."

His first thought was that he wouldn't tell Sarah.


HE AND PAUL TOOK A long train ride and then walked from the station through what looked like suburban streets. New houses with satellite dishes and painted garden elves had been built right up against the walls of the camp. He spent six hours inside, peering into the barracks, the prison yard, the infirmary, the pit for mass executions, the remains of the crematorium. In almost every building an enormous amount of information was displayed on large panels that could be pushed aside like leaves in a giant book: historical timelines, biographies of inmates, reproduced documents, far more than he could read in a dozen visits. No horror was softened, no cruelty excused. There had been no children and families here, thank God, but instead political dissidents, Jewish radicals, captured Soviet soldiers. He read about a German arrested and brought to the camp for being a homosexual. There was a photograph of him from before the war, a man with short hair happily posing in a dress and high heels in front of a doorway. Bernie found himself almost unable to look away from it, perhaps because it seemed so ordinary and comforting.

PAUL HAD KEPT A DISCREET distance from him during the visit, disappearing altogether for long stretches, and only reappeared by his side when he returned to the entrance. As they began their walk back to the station, Paul said, "If you will excuse this suggestion, perhaps you should have something to eat. It has been a long day without food or drink."

"No, that's all right. I'll have something back at the hotel."

They rode the train and took a cab to the hotel. Bernie insisted on giving Paul money for a ride home. Then he went up to his room and ordered a sandwich from room service. Even after taking a shower, he felt as if his skin were covered in ash. He did not want Sarah to ask him about it. There was a knock on the door and he called, "Come in, I left it open." The waiter pushed in the cart covered in a white cloth and with a silver lid over his sandwich. In his robe, Bernie walked towards the cart, felt flush, then nauseous, and the ground rolled up from under him.

THE HOSPITAL KEPT HIM OVERNIGHT, not because of the bruise on his temple, but for his low blood sugar and slightly elevated heart rate. "Just to be on the safe side," the doctor said in English, looking over his glasses. Bernie decided not to call Sarah right away. His health plan allowed for a private room, but he slept fitfully, aggravated by the intravenous drip, vaguely aware of the occasional presence of the night nurse, longing for Ida. He was grateful when the sky began to lighten and finally the breakfast tray arrived. Only after he ate did he pick up the telephone.

It was less than half an hour before Sarah hurried into the room, Paul following behind her. She looked a mess, her face pale and her eyes almost wild.

"Zeyde, Zeyde, are you all right?" She leaned over the bed to hug him.

"Yes, yes, it's nothing. Paul was right, I needed to eat, that was all. You don't have to worry."

"I want to speak to the doctor," Sarah said. "Did you see a specialist? You absolutely have to see a specialist."

To Paul he said, "She takes after the women in the family."

"Oh, Zeyde, I should have gone with you. I don't know what's wrong with me."

"No," he said. "It's good you didn't. That would have been unbearable, darling."

HE WAS NOT RELEASED UNTIL the middle of the afternoon. They went to a restaurant across the street from the hospital, a real German place, the menu heavy with pork, sausage, and beef dishes, and everything accompanied by *Kartoffel*. But he only had soup and a little fish. Afterwards they took him to the hotel by taxi and although Sarah wanted to stay for the evening, he shooed them out. She made him promise that he would stay put until the morning when she would come to spend his last day with him. "That's an easy promise to make," he said, smiling at her.

She arrived at his hotel prepared to spend a quiet day in his room, or perhaps to take a little stroll. But he was ready to go out, guidebook in pocket. "I haven't seen the highlights yet. The Reichstag, Checkpoint Charlie. What's left of the wall."

"I don't want you getting tired, Zeyde."

"So we'll splurge on a cab or two."

As they walked she took his arm. He felt his heart lighten with the warmth of her. Just her presence made him feel happy. At lunch, she leaned towards him and said, "I like it here, Zeyde. And I feel guilty about liking it. But sometimes I'm uncomfortable, too. I get really spooked. It's like, the things growing here are beautiful, but under the earth there's blood feeding the roots. I feel conflicted all the time. About Paul, too. I look down at my feet, I see one of those little bronze markers, that a Jewish person lived there, the date of his or her deportation, and I think, what am I doing here? When you announced that you were coming and just the idea of you being here freaked me out. And then going to Sachsenhausen. I've been meaning to go myself, I almost did a month ago, but every time I try ..."

She just shook her head. He put his hand — bony, liver-spotted — over hers. "I'll tell you something. Something different, I mean. You want to know how your grandmother and I met?"

She looked confused by his change of subject, but she said, "Yes, please."

"In a dream."

"Excuse me?"

"I was working in the office of a jewellery store on King

Street. One night I dreamed a woman came in. As soon as I saw her I knew that we were destined to be husband and wife. Of course it was just a dream and I didn't think anything of it. But then a month later, I was talking on the telephone to a customer and a woman walked in — the same woman as in the dream. Ida. I didn't tell her though, not until after we were engaged. I was afraid she would think I was crazy."

"I don't believe it! What could it mean?"

He shrugged. "She died in her sleep, you know. In bed, beside me. I've been very lucky in my life."

IN THE MORNING, THE AUTOMATIC telephone call woke him. Getting out of bed, he felt sore on his left side from the fall. He washed, dressed in the newly pressed suit, and waited for the bellboy to come and fetch his suitcase.

He stood outside the glass doors of the hotel while the doorman walked to the street to flag a taxi. The morning was cold and bright. All that waited for him on the other side of the ocean was an empty house with the thermostat turned down. The driver opened the trunk and put in the suitcase. The cab door was open, but he hesitated a moment longer and, sure enough, he heard Sarah's voice calling. He saw her hurrying across the square, hair loose, looking so wonderfully young and alive. She bounded up the stairs and now she was hugging him hard, her face wet, saying into his ear, "I'm really, really happy you came, Zeyde. I'm just so glad."

He tried to laugh but found himself suppressing a sob instead. "I am too, sweetheart. But you know what? I never finished the Heinrich Böll. It was good, but it was beyond me."

# My Life among the Apes

FOR NEARLY A YEAR I lived among the apes. I knew by sight more than two dozen chimpanzees living by Lake Tanganyika in the remote Gombe Stream Game Reserve. Goliath, the alpha male. David Greybeard. Rudolph. Flo. I was among those who first saw a chimp make and use a tool — a twig stripped of its leaves and thrust into the hole of a termite hill. Once a mother held her infant out for me to groom. Once I witnessed a colony of chimps surround a stray member of another tribe and commit murder.

And then I gave it all up.

HOFFSTEDDER IS ON MY CASE again. First, someone in the branch has been using an anonymous blog to write slurs about management. Second, for reasons unexplained, the number of after-hour deposits at our ATM has declined by four percent. Third, a passcard has gone missing.

I am fifty-one years old and have not risen as far as others my age, but I came to banking late, after an unfinished Ph.D. and careers in housing management and commercial liability insurance. The best that I can say about banking is that I like the people I work with (all except Hoffstedder) and I can walk to work in forty minutes.

The staff under me, tellers and assistant managers, are fifteen to twenty-five years younger. They are first and second-generation sons and daughters of India, Pakistan, Portugal, Iran, the Azores. They are inexpensively but sharply dressed. Both sexes wear earrings, but other visible piercings are not permitted while at work. Little indentations can be seen, by an eyebrow, a lip, where a stud or ring has been removed. They spend their lunch hours text messaging their friends. On Monday mornings they look wasted from weekend raves, or whatever it is they do. The younger ones seem to form no permanent relationships but have a lot of sex. They live two worlds away from my own, and I wish them well.

ONE DAY WHEN I was eleven, I came home to find the latest *National Geographic* on the kitchen counter, along with a glass of milk and a wedge of burnt-sugar cake. I opened it and saw a beautiful, young blond woman washing her hair in a stream.

"Don't disappear with that magazine," my mother warned me as I slipped off the stool. "Nobody else has seen it yet."

We lived in the suburb of Willowdale. I had my own room while my older brothers shared one. A desk, a bookcase, a *World Book Encyclopedia*, a telescope. I was short for my age, and overweight. I dreaded gym class. Two girls down the street tormented me every day on the way home. In the evening we watched *Rowan and Martin's Laugh-In*.

But that night I began to live in the jungle.

MY WIFE, LIZETTE, IS A teacher in a private girl's school. Even when we met, over two decades ago, her anxiousness made it hard for her to see a movie or attend a party where there might be strangers. Not until after our third child was old enough for Lizette to go back to work part-time did the true panic attacks begin. She had to take a medical leave and endure hours of fitfully successful therapy before the proper dosage of a new drug began to help. Medication has made life more tolerable for her, although I became the one who took our boys to hockey practice and attended our daughter's piano recitals.

I still find myself frustrated and angry that we cannot go on holidays, or to the theatre, or to a dinner party. Two years ago I conceived the idea of visiting France for my fiftieth birthday, but of course we could not go. I fantasize about going on my own (and having an affair with a beautiful woman), but along with the fantasy comes guilt and shame, which results in my treating Lizette with an excessive delicacy that annoys her.

FOR MY SCIENCE PRESENTATION THE year I was eleven, I chose Jane Goodall's research on primate behaviour. I stood before the class and talked about how as a young girl she had written down her observations of birds and animals around her home, then as a young woman how she had become secretary to the famous paleontologist Louis Leakey, who was looking for someone to study chimpanzees in the wild. I spoke of her findings: how chimps slept in nests that they made by bending branches down with their feet, how grooming was an important form of social interaction. I passed around photographs.

Two photographs I kept to myself. One was Jane Goodall washing her hair. The other was a close-up of her in profile looking into the face of a chimp. Her own eyes blue, her lips slightly parted. That night in bed, I imagined writing to Jane Goodall and telling her of my admiration for her work. At the same time, I modestly pointed out something that she had missed but that I noticed from the photographs, an observation about the way chimpanzees communicate with gestures. I sent the letter to her care of the offices of the National Geographic Society and in a short time I received a telegram which the delivery man read while my family stood by the door and listened.

BRILLIANT OBSERVATION STOP HAVE UNFILLED ASSISTANT POSITION STARTING IMMEDIATELY STOP YOU ARE URGENT- LY NEEDED STOP PLANE TICKET ARRIVING TOMORROW STOP JANE GOODALL

My parents and my brothers stared at me in stunned amazement. Finally my dad said, "Well, son, you better get packing."

I EMAIL A REPORT ABOUT the missing passcard to Hoffstedder. Our newest and youngest teller, Kate Sulimani, accidentally took it home. Her boyfriend hid it as a prank and when Kate found out and demanded it back, he couldn't find it. They think it ended up in the recycled trash but as its destruction can't be proven I have taken the precaution of recalling all the passcards and ordering replacements with new codes.

Hoffstedder's reply is two words: "Fire her." I write back, explaining that this is Kate Sulimani's first job out of community college, that staff members have occasionally forgotten to leave their passcards, and that she understands the gravity of her error.

He writes back again. "I said fire her."

I have no choice but to call her into my office. She leaves in tears. When I come out to get a coffee, the other tellers will not look at me.

Before Christmas two months ago, Kate Sulimani drew my name. At the party she gave me a tie. You have to look very closely at the pattern to see that it is made up of little Homer Simpsons. I happen to be wearing that tie today.

I bring my coffee back to my desk and look for something to put it down on. I find the scrap of newspaper that I ripped out of the *Globe* a few days ago, the notice that Jane Goodall is coming to give a talk. She is on a fundraising mission for a group that wants to build a retirement sanctuary for old research chimps. Tickets are fifty dollars.

AT HOME I LISTEN TO a phone message from our older son. He isn't coming home from school this weekend after all. I put the phone down and look for his brother to shoot some baskets until I remember that his band is having a rehearsal in the drummer's garage. Our daughter is at her boyfriend's.

Lizette comes downstairs and as I open a bottle of Zinfandel, she starts chopping vegetables.

At the stove, Lizette says, "I see that Jane Goodall is coming to town."

"Uh-huh."

"She hasn't phoned you?"

"Very funny."

"Maybe we can go."

"Really, it's okay."

THE FOLLOWING WINTER I BEGAN studying for my Bar Mitzvah. Some kids I knew developed an intense fervour about their Jewishness. They started wearing yarmulkes.

I was thinking about chimpanzees in the context of evolutionary theory.

On the day of my Bar Mitzvah, I wore a double-breasted suit with a light pink shirt and a blue tie. The synagogue was crowded with guests for me and also for a girl named Denise who was having her Bat Mitzvah. She read her portion flawlessly as was required, while I stumbled three times and the rabbi made me stop and repeat each word correctly.

Denise gave her talk first and then it was my turn. I was supposed to give an explanation of my Torah portion and draw from it a moral lesson. But I began by leaning into the microphone and quoting an earlier biblical passage: *And Jacob said to Rebekah his mother, Behold, Essau my brother is a hairy man, and I am a smooth man.*

FIRING KATE SULIMANI HAS DAMAGED branch morale. The tellers resent losing their friend and feel insecure in their own jobs. I consider holding a staff meeting to discuss the matter but decide that I have nothing to offer, that all I would be doing is asking them to still see me as a nice guy.

I did not consider refusing to fire her. I have college bills to pay, the mortgage, the usual. What is Kate Sulimani to me? She's young and will bounce back. She has her whole life ahead of her.

In the bathroom mirror, I see the beginning of pouches under my eyes, sagging jowls. I look the part I am playing: Hoffstedder's man.

IN HIGH SCHOOL, I SMOKED a lot of dope, drank on weekends, bet on American football through a kid in history class who worked for a bookie. I read books on Buddhism, or first chapters of books. I failed two courses.

One day in the middle term of grade twelve, I found out that I had to present a project in biology that I hadn't known about — hadn't known because I'd skipped a week of classes. At home, I looked through our Time-Life Science books hoping for something I could pull together. Then I remembered my old Jane Goodall project. I found it stuffed in the bottom drawer and when I pulled out the file, the photograph of Jane Goodall washing her hair fell out. It seemed to me that I could pretty much recycle the old material, adding in details as I remembered them, but that I would need to make it longer. So I got out my portable cassette recorder, plugged in the microphone, and began to make chimp calls.

Imitating chimpanzees that I had heard on television documentaries had been all that remained from my Jane Goodall period. In a car with friends, at parties, walking at

night with my buddies, I would begin with low hoots and
then break into louder barks and howls. Everyone always
said how real they sounded and I knew that Mr. Anderson,
my dim-witted biology teacher who wore his hair long
and liked to act chummy with us, wouldn't know the difference. The next day in class, I gave my presentation,
embellishing as I went along, and then explained how I had
obtained a tape recording by writing to the National Geographic Society. I pressed the "play" button of the recorder.
Every so often I paused it to explain the meaning of a call:
anger, frustration, submission, fear, loneliness. Finally, I
turned the recorder off and said that despite the fact that
human beings had built cities, flown to the moon, and
invented surface-to-air missiles, the difference between us
and apes might only be a matter of degree.

Mr. Anderson looked at me a long moment and then said,
"Get to the office."


BROODING BEHIND MY DESK, I recall a long-forgotten detail.
I don't remember whether it was in that first *National
Geographic* or one of the television specials that came after.
How an adult male chimpanzee named Mike stole the domi-
nant male position. The previous alpha male, Goliath, was
huge and powerful, and the smaller Mike was no match
for him. But Mike found two empty petrol cans in Jane
Goodall's camp. He learned to bash them forward as he
ran, making an awful racket that terrified the other chimps,
including Goliath. When Mike finally stopped, Goliath
came over and, grunting in supplication, reached out to
groom Mike's fur. Mike became the alpha male.

All I need is some petrol cans to bash. I'm not sure if what I have in mind is equivalent, but it's close enough. I pick up the phone.

"Hoffstedder here."

"Stanley, it's Allen."

"You figured out why your ATM numbers are down?"

"I'm working on it. Listen, Stan, about that teller we let go. I've got a rep from the Civil Liberties Union coming here tomorrow. He's asking about discrimination, unfair practises, even about going to the media. If I tell him what I really think —"

"Are you squeezing my balls, Allen?"

"No, of course not. But when he asks me —"

"You'll know what to tell him, won't you? That the girl was incompetent and posed a risk to our clients and that we gave her the standard package. I don't want to hear any more about it. Now on those ATM numbers, you check if a homeless guy's been sleeping in your doorway at night, keeping the customers away. Happens all the time."

I hear the sound of the click at the other end.

AT HOME, I SAY TO Lizette, "Are the kids never coming home for dinner? Maybe we should just set up a trust fund for them."

She dishes scalded rapini with feta, next to the sole on my plate. "We're boring to them. It's natural. And they've all promised to be home tomorrow. The only real problem is that you're bored of me."

"Likely the other way around. I wouldn't blame you. I feel like I've become nothing but my job."

"I have a present for you. Just a small one, so don't get too excited."

"What is it?"

"Look under your plate."

"I feel like I'm twelve," I say, shifting my plate over. Underneath is a ticket. Jane Goodall at Convocation Hall.

"It's in an hour," she says. "You better eat up."

"Just me?"

"I'm sorry. I'm just not up to it right now."

"Sure." I get up and kiss her. "Thanks."

I sit down again and we start to eat.

THE LAST TIME I WAS in Convocation Hall was to receive the diploma for my undergraduate degree. About all I could remember was what a bad hangover I'd had. Now I look down to the stage to see Jane Goodall behind the slender Plexiglas podium. Behind her a large screen shows a series of video clips. She no longer looks like the slim woman washing her hair in an African stream. She is a handsome older woman, comfortably filled out, a quaver in her voice. A good speaker, if overly rehearsed, as if she has given this same speech a thousand times.

After the talk, I buy one of her books and line up to have it signed. We shuffle forward, waiting for our turn at the table where she sits with pen in hand. As we get closer I feel increasingly agitated. At last it is my turn and as I move up she looks at me.

It takes me a moment to speak. "Ms. Goodall, I've been an admirer of yours since I was a boy."

"Have you? How very nice." She smiles wearily, as if she

has met many like me and knows all our secrets. "Shall I sign it to you?"

"No," I say. "To a friend of mine. Kate Sulimani. I'll spell it."

KATE SULIMANI LIVES IN A high-rise apartment in a cluster of six buildings off the Don Valley Parkway. An empty green space with a dry fountain in the middle. It looks like some invented city, Brasilia maybe. I look for the name on the directory and press the button.

"Hello?"

"Kate, it's Allen Wernick."

The buzzer sounds and the door unlocks. The lobby of her building smells of bleach. I take the elevator up, reading the notices taped to the bulletin board: nanny available, lost cat, whoever stole my bike please return it no questions asked. When I get off at the seventh floor, she's already at her door, holding it open about three inches. She wears a cotton robe. From inside I can hear music, some techno thing.

"What do you want, Mr. Wernick? Are you here to give me my job back?"

"I wish I was. I really just want to say that I'm sorry. You weren't treated fairly."

"Yeah, well, life sucks that way."

"I've written a letter of recommendation for you."

"You can do that?"

"I don't know, actually. Anyway, here, it's inside this book. The book is for you, too."

I hold out the book with the letter sticking out from

between its pages. She looks at it a moment before taking it. Then she stares at the cover.

"The woman who lives with monkeys, right?"

"Chimpanzees, actually."

She opens the book to the title page. "It's signed."

"Yes."

"'To a fellow animal lover'?"

"I guess that's what she always writes."

"A bit weird but thanks, I guess."

"Don't mention it."

I take a step back and Kate Sulimani closes the door.

I PARK THE CAR AT the curb and turn off the ignition. In the dark I rest my head against my arms on the steering wheel. I feel tired, but it isn't the good sort of tired that comes from a long walk. I get out of the car and lock it with the remote key, making the lights flash.

I enter the side door as quietly as I can, but Lizette is still up, sitting at the kitchen table in a cotton nightgown. The cake we didn't have time to eat is on the table.

"How was it?"

"Good," I say. "She's a woman who knows her chimps."

"Is she older too or is it just us?"

I lean over and kiss her. "You're very beautiful."

She shrugs me off. " Do you want a piece of cake?"

"Hmm."

She cuts a slice and puts it on a plate, slides it to me as I sit down. I take a bite. "It's delicious." I took another. "I don't like firing people."

The next few bites I eat without tasting and then the slice

is gone. I want to go to bed but I can't move. Lizette doesn't move either and I become aware of the ticking of the clock on the wall.

"I think we should go on a holiday this year," she says.

All right, I say. At least, I think I say it. I'm not sure, but I don't say it again.

# The Creech Sisters

THE SUMMER THE CREECH SISTERS tried to seduce my father turned out to be the last that we spent on the island. It was a very small island in Georgian Bay, all eight cottages clustered near the beach, ours closest to the water and the one belonging to Mrs. Creech the farthest. To reach the island we had to take a ten-minute boat ride. There were a couple of men on the mainland who used their boats as unofficial taxis for the cottagers. Mrs. Creech, who was not only heavy but an invalid (a word still used forty years ago), had to be lifted in and out of a boat by her two daughters. Three or four kids always hung around gawking, just in case the boat finally capsized and Mrs. Creech was plunged into the lake.

During this fourth island summer I had no inkling it would be the last and so no sadness or first taste of nostalgia. I am in my early fifties now; that July I was twelve-and-a-half, a middle son. My brothers were fourteen and nine and the three of us had already explored the island with a freedom that we were not allowed back in the city. The interior rose gradually and stunted evergreens grew up between the rock plates. We sometimes found the remains of a campfire, or a shotgun-blasted coffee can, or a condom. The night was especially eerie because in the city there was no real darkness, while here the night skies were awash with stars. I never had bad dreams sleeping in the cottage, as I often did in Toronto, perhaps because at the end of those long days in the fresh air I was simply too tired.

MY FATHER DIDN'T LIKE BEING in the country. Born in Warsaw, he had spent his youth in Vienna, Brussels, Paris — wherever his merchant father took his family. He had entered Canada on a student visa in 1942, Jewish refugees no longer being permitted into the country, and was proud to have been the youngest graduating lawyer in his class. In the years that followed he lost his accent (although there was a non-native's precision to his speech) but never his European air of sophistication. He was the only father I knew who liked to wear his overcoat draped on his shoulders, and when as a young adult I finally did see someone else looking so suave it was Jean-Paul Belmondo in a French film. My father was short but did not seem to know it, and he had a beautiful ease with people that I was just beginning to notice. Women were especially drawn to him. I once had a French teacher named Mrs. Lupenski who loved to hear his Parisian accent when he spoke French and once, in front of my class, called him a "dreamboat."

My father thrived on the pleasures and obligations of city life, and spending three weeks on the island was like waiting out a prison sentence. He needed newspapers and magazines, opera, cocktail parties. He loved to take my mother to expensive restaurants where there was a band for dancing. But he had been given the right of occupancy of the cottage when one of his clients could not pay his legal bill. I'm sure my father would have preferred to forgive the debt, but when my mother heard about the offer she insisted that we take it.

My mother never liked the city, although by then she had already lived in Toronto for almost twenty years. She was a small-town Episcopalian who met my father in the University of Toronto infirmary, where she was a volunteer nurse to the new army recruits being billeted in tents on the campus lawns. Her parents had been against her going for fear that she would be undone by some private about to be shipped overseas, but instead she fell for my father. He came into the infirmary with one eye swollen shut, having hit himself with a badminton racquet while playing in the Hart House gymnasium.

Even if my father had wanted to practise law in my mother's home town, as a Jew he would not have found many clients. So she got used to the city, taking us to visit her parents every Christmas where a tree and presents awaited. My father always stayed home, to clear up paperwork, he claimed. When my mother sometimes brought up the subject of buying a cottage he always said that it would be just another property to look after when he hardly had time to take care of the house. Actually, he didn't take care of the house at all; it was my mother who called the plumber or electrician when something needed fixing.

When the offer of the cottage came up, he could think of no good reason to refuse her.

IN THE EARLY MORNINGS MY mother took her coffee down to the beach to watch the sun play over the water. Then she roused everyone out of bed and made pancakes or French toast, which we ate while still in our pyjamas. During the day she went for walks with my father or alone, watched us swim, baked pies in the wood stove. In the very late afternoon when the beach was usually deserted, she went for her own swim, doing the crawl out to the floating deck and back several times. She was not fast, but she had a fine form, as my father liked to remark, and hardly left a ripple on the surface. She would walk dripping onto the beach again and, ignoring our pleas of hunger, take a shower as she hummed to herself before dressing again to finish dinner.

My father appreciated her contentedness, even if he couldn't stop himself from pacing the small cottage rooms, picking up and putting down the days-old newspaper, going outside in the hope of finding someone to talk to. Every few days he would take the boat back to the mainland and spend a couple of hours on the phone to his secretary and various clients, after which he would be calmer for a while. My mother said that he didn't have to stay with us for the whole three weeks, that he could go back for the middle week, but he wouldn't hear of it. At the time I thought it was because he didn't want to leave my brothers and me. He played Monopoly and Clue with us and soccer games on the beach.

I realize now that he didn't go because he didn't like to be away from my mother.

THE CREECH SISTERS WERE HARDLY old but they were "mature girls," as my father called them. Ellen, the elder sister, was past forty and Louise was three or four years younger. Unlike my mother, they both had jobs, Ellen as a veterinarian's assistant and Louise as a speech therapist, one of the first in the province. Both of them continued to live with their mother, which *my* mother said was the root of their problem. I couldn't exactly see that they had a problem except for their rather plain faces and that they seemed to smile only as a nervous habit. My father, who knew my mother was one quarter Scots, joked that they had dour Scots blood and *that* was the root of their problem.

Despite my always thinking of them as a pair, the Creech sisters were not quite so alike as all that. Ellen seemed more sombre and uneasy around people; she usually walked on the paths between the cottages with her eyes cast down. She had long black hair that she kept done up unless it was wet. When my father greeted her, remarking on the "sumptuous" weather or asking if she had seen the Canada Geese overhead, honking like "Manhattan taxi-cabs," she always blushed. Louise, the younger, was not quite so timid. She sometimes chatted with my father and seemed to feel at ease with him. Louise had the better figure and moved in a more feminine manner, although both sisters were busty and wide-hipped. I tried not to appear to watch them when they took Mrs. Creech down to the beach in her wheelchair and then splashed about in the shallows. I sometimes had to tear my eyes away from Louise's very white thighs. Once my mother put her hand on my shoulder and said if I had nothing better to do she knew of plenty of chores around the cottage.

Some nights, I didn't fall asleep immediately. Instead, I lay in bed and thought about the Creech sisters and became hard. I was still a couple of months away from discovering how to relieve my own arousal and just lay on my side, towards the wall and away from my brothers, and tried to keep still. It never occurred to me that my older brother might have similar thoughts. He never looked at the Creech Sisters. I suppose if there had been any teenage girls on the island, we would have had crushes on them, but there were only little kids. So the Creech sisters became the object of my rapt attention and reveries. No doubt that was why what they did to my father seemed so exciting and lurid and appalling.

IT RAINED ONLY ONE AFTERNOON during those three weeks. The sky clouded over and the rain came almost instantly, a true downpour. We fled up from the beach, screaming with pleasure, and stood breathlessly on the porch as the lake vanished in the mist. Inside, my mother said that the sun was waiting behind the clouds and the storm wouldn't last long. So my brothers and I started a game of Monopoly, which I always lost because my older brother managed to trade me out of my best properties. Only my father was missing; he had gone wandering off as usual and my mother was starting to look concerned when the door opened and he came in, soaked to the skin, half-covered in mud, his face flushed from the exertion of running.

"Don't you come in with those wet clothes," she commanded, and while he stripped on the mat she brought him a towel and robe. Then he fell into a beat-up easy chair and said to no one in particular, "Well, the damnedest thing just happened to me."

This was not my father's usual mode of expression, which was why I turned my head away from the game board to look at him again. He was trying to sound folksy to indicate that whatever had happened ought not be taken too seriously. I cannot remember precisely any of his other words; instead, I can "see" what he described almost as if I had witnessed it myself, no doubt because of the countless times I imagined the scene afterwards.

My father had been taking a walk and, preoccupied with one of his client's legal problems, hadn't noticed the clouds overhead. When the rain began he was a hundred or so yards beyond the last cottage, wandering among the small stand of birch trees that were scarred by kids pulling off the bark. He started to run, but he was almost instantly soaked through and, peering through the rain, he saw Louise Creech waving to him from the back window of her cottage. There must have been a lamp on for him to see her.

The Creech sisters often asked my father to do small favours around the cottage, since neither of them, as Louise said, was "very handy." While he himself had virtually no practical skills, my father's pride did not allow him to admit it, so he would go off with a screwdriver or wrench from the toolkit the restaurant owner kept under the sink and come home again looking triumphant for not having made the problem worse. Well, he saw Louise Creech wave from the window and he ran through the rain to the front of the cottage and up the slippery porch steps. Louise opened the door. She was wearing a raincoat and he guessed that she had been about to come fetch him. Their mother was napping, she said, and then told him that a leak had started in the roof above the sisters' bedroom and they didn't know what to do. "How about praying for the rain to stop?" my father joked, but Louise didn't smile and he followed her inside. He took off his shoes and socks, whispering that he would be just a moment, and this time Louise giggled. "You don't have to whisper," she said. "When our mother naps she's dead to the world on account of the painkillers."

She took him down the hall, past Mrs. Creech's closed door behind which he could hear her snoring as deeply as a man, to the bedroom at the end. The door was ajar and Louise paused in the narrow hall so that my father would enter first. When he did the first thing he saw was the elder sister, Ellen, lying naked on the nearest bed. She was on her back and her eyes were closed, her arms at her side and her large breasts flattened by gravity. Without opening her eyes, Ellen said something. "Bake me" was how it sounded to my father, although after he realized she must have said, "Take me." Looking down on her, my father was at a loss what to do. I don't believe he felt any sexual stirring at all, not the way I did when I later imagined the scene. He turned to the younger sister for help only to see that Louise had let the raincoat slip from her shoulders. She wore only a pair of white underpants. She looked right into my father's eyes and smiled.

I don't think he got a good look at Louise because she

was standing so close to him. I do remember what he told us next:

"I got the hell out of there."

Which he did. It was his lawyer's instinct not to be caught in a compromising situation. Mumbling a pardon under his breath, he carefully edged past Louise and almost sprinted in his bare feet down the hall. He stuffed his wet socks into his pocket, stuck his feet into his squelching shoes, and was out the door. He slipped on the stairs and though he managed to grab the rail he still landed on his behind, bruising his tailbone. On the sloping path to our cottage he slipped a second time, going down in the mud. He slowed a little for the rest of the way, although I don't think he felt safe until our door was closed behind him.

ONLY YEARS LATER DID IT occur to me to wonder whether my father ought to have told my mother, or if he needed to, why he didn't wait until they were alone. Why, in front of his three young sons, would he relate an amusing little story out of two women trying to seduce him? Perhaps he thought that the more witnesses to his story the better. Or that if he made light of it in our presence, our mother would see it the same way. Perhaps he believed us too young to know what he was talking about. Or simply wasn't thinking. My younger brother certainly didn't listen and my older brother gave no reaction. As for my mother, she stopped kneading the bread dough on the table, but did not look up. Her face had gone as white as the flour on her hands. When my father finished speaking, she washed up in the kitchen sink, took off her apron, and went into their bedroom, shutting the door behind her. The ball of dough sat on the table for the rest of the day and into the next morning, when I tentatively poked my finger through the hardened skin that had formed over the still-soft centre.

THE RAIN DID NOT RETURN, but it might just as well have. A pall seemed to fall over our cottage. My younger brother noticed the least, although even he seemed subdued in his play. My older brother began spending more time alone, walking along the shore and poking a stick under rocks. While my father pretended to be his cheerful self, I could see he was concerned about my mother. I often caught him looking at her; sometimes he would go up to whisper something in her ear or try to take her around the waist, and she would turn passive, neither responding nor pulling away. He did not take the boat to the mainland again, as if afraid to leave her. Before this I had no awareness that my parents had a private life, an ongoing emotional drama that existed separately from their relations with us.

I could not understand what my mother was upset about. After all, my father had refused the Creech sisters and had even told us about it. When we saw the sisters now, which was unavoidable, he alone greeted them as he had always done. My mother seemed to blame him, as if he was not only responsible but had given in to the temptation. Otherwise, why would she look so wounded?

My own feelings about what had happened were decidedly confused. I found thinking about it far too exciting to be wholly glad that my father had refused. Or maybe I wished that it had happened to my father, except that he wasn't my father but someone else, such as me ten years in the future. I just couldn't help wanting to know what exactly might have happened if the person who wasn't my father, who was me, hadn't run away. The possibility of one man and two women had never occurred to me. On one hand it seemed almost a waste, considering that I could barely imagine dealing satisfactorily with one. But on the other hand ... well. In some way I was disappointed by my father's honourable retreat. How could he not have felt his resolve weaken in the presence of Ellen Creech, amazingly naked on the bed, her black hair undone (as I pictured it) and fanning out around her head. Or Louise Creech in her underpants (which I had seen hanging on the washing line), gazing into his eyes? If I was my father I would not have been able to resist. I would have kissed Louise on the mouth and put my hand on her breast. I would have lain down on top of Ellen even in my wet clothes!

At the end of the week our holiday was over and we went home again. Then my parents did something that I could remember them doing only once before: they went on a trip without us. A woman named Mrs. Kratzuk came to stay with us for what seemed like a month, but couldn't have been more than a few days. She was a vile cook and we survived largely on bread and peanut butter. I can't remember where they went, only that my father arranged it all and that my mother — as he expected — resisted going but finally gave in.

When they came home, bearing expensive gifts for us, my mother was happy. She seemed to have fallen in love with my father all over again. I didn't realize it then, but I see now that the real seduction took place not at the cottage but during those few days away. Or perhaps not really a seduction, but a patient and persistent courtship. I wonder if they felt — despite whichever first-class hotel they stayed in — a little like their younger selves, when my father lived in an ill-kept boarding house and my mother in a dormitory and they reached out to each other in need.

The following summer we went to Montreal for our holiday, where we visited art galleries and went to nice restaurants and my father bantered in French with the waiters. I assumed that my mother had forbidden our return to the cottage, but in fact the owner had managed to pay off his bill and took the property back from us.

FORTY YEARS LATER, MY MOTHER is dead and my father mourns for her in his retirement. Both my brothers have taken after my father; they are lawyers, the elder a law professor, as well as loyal husbands and devoted fathers. Why I turned out differently is the haunting question of my life, but it is perhaps the reason that I remember this incident, which my brothers both claim to have forgotten.

A small detail of our last leaving of the island has recently come back to me. One of the boats came to take us back to the mainland and we filled it with suitcases and boxes. The wind had picked up, making the water a little choppy. I held tightly onto the side of the boat as the man stood in the shallows in his rubber boots and pushed us off. Looking back at the island, I saw Ellen and Louise Creech, standing by a spruce tree that had been split by lightning years ago. They were watching us. My mother must have seen them, too, for I heard her say quietly, "Those poor girls."

I wonder why I forgot that last sight of them for so long. Perhaps I didn't want to think of them as pitiable, for that would have spoiled the imagining that played over and over in my head. Recalling my mother's voice now, it is clear to me that she never really doubted my father's loyalty or believed him responsible. She must have been upset by deeper feelings of inadequacy, the sort that she suffered from all her life and that could be triggered by a seemingly harmless word from my father. I feel no disappointment in my father now, only admiration for the way he knew what was good in his life and what he wanted most. And I think of the Creech sisters, those poor girls. What they were hoping for and what they didn't find.

# The Brooklyn Revenge

I GOT MYSELF A NICE little sublet on Ninth Street between Avenues A and B in the East Village. It was about ten steps from Thompkins Square Park. I remember reading how the park had been turned into a squatters' village, homeless people or maybe drunks and addicts living in taped-together shacks until Mayor Dinkins bulldozed them out. Anyway, now Thompkins Square Park was all winding paths between the lush green flora, constantly tended by gardeners, although certain benches were occupied most of the day by runaway kids with their knapsacks and guitars and skinny dogs. I liked sitting in the park with a book of poems or my notebook and a take-out coffee, like an old hippy who'd always lived there.

I was sixty-one years old and preferred Birkenstocks, Indian skirts, narrow-strapped tops that showed off my shoulder blades. My friends always said that I looked like a refugee from some hipper time and place. And, different as New York was, I felt immediately at home. Even at night, the sirens and car horns and drunken singing made me feel safer than those dark and empty lawns.

My name is Cleo Dunkelman. I had been a widow going on fourteen months. A mother of three grown children, grandmother of two. A part-time bookkeeper, now retired. I had come to New York for what my oldest daughter, my most exasperating child, insisted on calling "revenge." I supposed she was right and to myself, if not to her, I began to call it "the Brooklyn Revenge," since it was going to take place across the river.

But I'm not quite ready to talk about that. First, I want to tell how, in New York, I became something else as well. A poet. Back in the late sixties in college (when, in fact, I wasn't a hippy but a good girl, going to class from my parents' house, dating Harry on Saturday nights) I took a few frivolous literature courses and fell unabashedly in love with poetry. A love which continued even after I married and quit my job when I became pregnant, and ran our house and raised the kids and kept the books for a couple of dozen small businesses, working at the dining room table. It was my pleasure and indulgence to buy a new poetry book, at first one of the classics, later one of the modern poets, someone I'd never heard of but who caught me with a title or a line, which was how I fell for a Swedish poet named Lars Gustafsson, a Hungarian named Dezso Tandori, a Canadian named Roo Borson. I didn't even have anywhere to put those sliver-thin books; they were piled on the floor by my side of the bed, stuffed between the cookbooks in the kitchen. As far as Harry was concerned, reading poetry was my hobby, equivalent to scrapbooking or learning to play the dulcimer. Maybe he felt it justified his hobby, too, which was cheating on me.

In all those years of making dinner and figuring out how to deduct a trip to Miami as a business expense, of running the kids to skating lessons and dance recitals, not one poem did I write. Poetry wasn't about expressing myself, but falling into someone else's words. I had no secret frustrated desire. But, in New York, the first time I left my apartment to go for a walk, I went into a stationery shop and bought a Moleskine notebook and a pen. I went into the park, sat on a bench, and immediately wrote a poem. I am not saying it was a good poem, or original, or worth anything. I'm not going to give it to you here to read, because I have no need. But I wrote three poems that day, two the next, and it kept going. I began taking my notebook into Café Orlins, which was two steps below the curb and so felt underground, and which is why I can say that besides everything else, besides being just another woman who was cheated on, I was also a poet.

I DIDN'T DISCOVER MY HUSBAND's affair until the day after his death, while looking through his papers for a file he kept on family history to give to the rabbi for the eulogy. I found a shoebox stuffed with nine years of letters from one Tilly Mellankop, who had liked to put a drop of perfume on her girly notepaper. *Here, use this,* I wanted to say to the rabbi, shoving a handful of letters smelling like air freshener at him. I resisted the urge, but at the funeral found myself violently throwing dirt onto the casket until somebody took the shovel away.

Tilly Mellankop was an executive secretary at Holtzman Sleepwear, but had retired six months before, as I found out on phoning the office. She was a divorcée, a word I thought should be brought back into fashion. There was only one T. Mellankop in the Brooklyn telephone directory. I would go across the river, all right. I would meet her when I was good and ready.

IT WAS SARAH, MY OLDEST, who gave me the cellphone. And she who called me every day.

"All right, Mom, enough is enough. It's time to come home."

It was as if she was trying to reverse our roles. I could imagine her moving about the house, just twelve blocks from my own, picking up kids' toys or maybe pulling things from the fridge to start dinner. My two younger ones were busy with their own messy adventures and called me every week or so. But Sarah, the one who tried so hard to replicate her parents' life as she saw it, made me want to scream.

"I know, sweetheart. It's hard not having me there. And nobody wants to see her mother enjoying herself."

"I hope you don't believe that. I'm worried about your safety. You could get mugged or worse, God forbid."

*God forbid?* She sounded like her late grandmother. "New York is safe these days, honey. And maybe you forgot about the home invasion around the corner from you? Or that pervert they haven't caught who goes through open windows and steals girls' underwear. I think we can manage a little separation for a while, Sarah. Your father was gone on his buying trips all the time."

"Okay, fine. If it's not about safety, then it's about your plan to see that woman. That's perverse. I know what Dad did was awful. I mean, if Gary ever tried, I'd run him over with the van. But Dad is gone. You don't need to demean yourself."

I looked out the window and saw two people carrying a rolled-up rug, like in *The Godfather*. "Sarah, you worry too much. I shouldn't have told you about it; that was a weak moment. I'm not going to demean myself. But I want to meet the woman who was part of your father's life for almost ten years. Who was expecting his next visit when he died."

"He never left you, Mom. Not in all that time."

"I wish he had," I said.

AFTER I HAD BEEN IN New York for a couple of weeks, and had filled one notebook with poems and then another with revisions, I passed a lamp post that someone had painted to look like an erect penis and noticed a flyer taped up. It was for an open writing workshop at the St. Mark's Poetry Project. I knew about the project, which had been run out of St. Mark's Church just over on Tenth Street since the sixties. The idea of attending intimidated me, but I was sixty-one years old. Nobody would expect much of me.

Wednesday night, as I walked over, I could feel my pulse throbbing. The desire to be noticed and praised never dies, I thought. Hand-drawn signs led me to a basement room where five women and three men sat at a table under fluorescent lights with their manuscripts in front of them. One of the men was the workshop leader. I figured myself to be the oldest by a good twelve years. I sat down and listened. Most of the poems weren't very good, but there was a line or stanza here and there that had something, that caught the ear. When my turn came, I opened my notebook and read three poems one after the other. They were shorter than everyone else's. They rhymed. They didn't sound anything like me and they weren't beautiful.

"To be honest, they kind of freak me out," said a black woman with dreadlocks.

"Really," said the youngest woman in the room, the beautiful girl with a round face and green eyes. "You're pretty dark for a grandmother."

Jackson, the workshop leader, had a North Carolina accent and a voice so quiet I had to lean in to hear. "Maybe it's a good thing, to be freaked out once in a while." Painfully fair-skinned, he had freckles lighter than most people's complexions. I guessed him to be in his late thirties, despite the prematurely old face, the wrinkles around his eyes and mouth, the hollow cobbler's chest. The workshop was supposed to be free for only the first session, but the next week and the week after he didn't ask me for money. It was after the third class that I asked him out for a drink.

He was reluctant to talk about himself, but after a couple of beers he told me that his father sold farm machinery and his mother bred dogs. That he'd gone to a state college, married his hometown sweetheart, taught high school, divorced and moved to New York. He had published two novels, now out of print, and had been working on a third for seven years. His job, as a copy editor for a legal publisher, he claimed not to mind. He had managed to get a small apartment in a massive subsidized artist complex on the west side.

Me, I was happy to talk. I filled him in, right down to the box of scented sex-talk letters. "I keep putting off going to see her. I'm just savouring the moment a little longer."

"Whatever you're expecting, something else will happen. It always does."

"I don't have a particular way for it to work out. I only know what I'll say to her when she opens that door. After that we can scream, tear each other's hair out, or she can start to cry and tell me how much she misses him. It's all good, as the kids say."

"You are an — an unusual woman."

"You mean for somebody my age?"

"No, I mean for a Canadian."

He smiled. I liked the way he smiled. I said, "After you're finished that beer maybe you want to see where I'm living."

THE BROWNSTONE WAS COVERED IN flaking pink paint. My apartment was on the third floor and with each upward step my bravado receded. No number of protein shakes or power walks or yoga classes could erase the twenty-two years between us. I had no idea whether Jackson even had the same idea as I did. And it was an idea rather than actual desire, which I hadn't felt for longer than I could remember and doubted would ever feel again. My hand trembled as I unlocked the door.

The young woman who held the lease was an NYU graduate student gone to France. I had liked living in these student digs, surrounded by somebody else's books and postcards and Post-it notes. It was a tiny L-shaped space tucked in the corner of the building, a postage-stamp living room, a tiny kitchen in the bend with miniature appliances, a bedroom behind a beaded curtain. The windows gave it good light during the day, although now the red neon sign from the Mexican restaurant across Ninth Street gave it the atmosphere of an opium den. If I thought living here had transformed me I realized at this moment that I was wrong, for I felt my suburban self pour back into the shell of my body.

I went straight to the bedroom and lit the student's scented candle. Jackson flinched as the beaded curtain strands rolled over him. Bless him, he immediately came up and kissed me. I pulled off his T-shirt. He was skinny and unmuscular and pale as an inner stalk of celery, but his skin was hot to the touch. He whispered in my ear, unbuttoning my shirt while backing me up to the bed.

This is enough detail, except to say that although I did not "finish," to use an expression that I've read in novels, everything was lovely. Afterwards, he lay back, catching his breath, and then leaned over to kiss me again. "You are very beautiful," he said, even quieter than usual.

I got up, pulling the sheet around me. "The last time I had a new lover," I said, "you were two years old."

"Is that what you're writing down?" He was watching me open my notebook.

"Something like that," I said and wrote *pale as an inner stalk of celery*. "How about we run across the street? I'm starving."

"You know," he said. "I might be younger than you, but I'm not exactly a boy."

"I know," I said.

"YOUR GRANDCHILDREN ARE STARTING TO forget you," my daughter said on the phone.

"I just sent them presents in the mail. That should help them remember." I shouldn't have used that tone, but I was becoming a little impatient.

"I've been thinking. You could come and live with us. We'll turn the study into a bedroom. It has that little bathroom next to it. You're living in that house all by yourself. We'd all love to have you."

I looked out the window and saw a man lowering cases of Corona from a truck. I felt angry at my daughter for treating me like some incontinent ninety-year-old and tried to understand why she needed to see me this way. Maybe there was something going on with her.

"Are you okay, Sarah? Is there something you want to talk about?"

There was a long pause. Then Sarah began to cry. "I don't know what it is. I feel like I'm drowning."

MY HUSBAND HAD BEEN IN the *shmatte* business, buying seconds — shirts with uneven sleeves or bad stitching, dresses with misprinted fabric — which he repackaged with his Penny King Clothiers label and sold to discount stores across Canada. Holtzman Sleepwear was one of his most dependable suppliers. I slept in their pyjamas. He must have met Tilly Mellankop on one of his frequent buying trips. He was a big man, Harry, with a high shiny fore-head, a wide chest, beefy hands. It was his good nature, his deep and easy laugh, which won people over and made him such a good salesman. It wasn't so hard to imagine a woman falling for him nor, in retrospect, Harry being flattered by it. He wouldn't have had any bad intentions, Harry never did. In all likelihood, if I had confronted him he would have thrown up his hands and insisted that he had no idea how any of it happened.

Meanwhile, Tilly Mellankop, unlike me, had known every-thing — that she was the mistress, the pleasure rather than the obligation. No doubt she waited eagerly for his visits, Harry breezing into the office with a handful of roses bought from a street vendor, a box of chocolates. Even now the woman had what I was denied, the luxury of missing him.

The day after Jackson and I went to bed for the third time, I took the L-Train, holding a strap while it rattled under the Hudson. Then a walk of three blocks to the apart-ment house, a mousy-brown building with no doorman. As I was peering at the directory a teenager with a skateboard came out and I grabbed the door before it closed. The vestibule smelled like egg salad. I rode the elevator up, blood coursing in my veins. I was frightened and excited and sick. The cage shuttered and let me out into a dim hall, the overhead lights missing bulbs. Almost every door had a peephole and a *mezuzah*. Harry had walked down this very carpet, a spring in his step, a boner in his pants. And then I was at the door, 807. The Brooklyn love nest. I knocked.

The wait was long. And then, ear almost touching the door, I heard something inside.

"Who is it?"

Who is it? I hadn't prepared myself for the question. I considered lying to be sure of getting inside but decided not to stoop. I wanted the high ground.

"Cleo Dunkelman. Harry's widow." But even as I spoke the locks turned. The door opened on a woman in a housecoat, wig slightly askew, face the colour of ash. She gagged and hurried back into the apartment. I heard her retching.

I stepped in and closed the door behind me. The old-fashioned telephone table, rubber mat for shoes, little framed painting of the Parthenon. Canned laughter came from a television in the sitting room. I saw the drawn curtains, smelled sickness.

I took a couple of steps further in. "When was the last treatment?" I asked.

Tilly Mellankop shuffled out of the bathroom, wiping her face with a towel. "What did you say your name was?"

THE OFFICIAL DIAGNOSIS WAS CARCINOMA of unknown primary, meaning the doctors couldn't find the original tumour, let alone try to cut it out or reduce its size. They could only treat the secondary sites, first a lymph node in the neck, then in a lung, giving her a little longer and temporarily reducing the pain. Her health insurance was lousy and she was using up savings that she had hoped to leave to her daughter, even though they didn't get along. She'd already had two hospital stays and didn't want to go back. I rooted around in the kitchen and found a can of minestrone. Waiting for it to heat up, I noticed dried spills on the stovetop, crumbs on the counter, jars left open. I poured the soup into a big cup and brought it to Tilly on the sofa. Between sips she asked me about Sarah and the boys. She knew the ages of the grandkids. I didn't — couldn't — say a word about the affair. Instead, she suggested we play a few hands of gin rummy. It was evening by the time I got up to go.

"When are you coming back?"

"I don't know."

"There's a list on the fridge. Things I need. Toilet paper, coffee. Down the block is the supermarket I go to. Don't use the kosher butcher, he's too expensive. If you come by noon you can take me to my naturopath."

"All right," I heard myself say.

"And maybe you'll bring something to read to me."

"Read to you?"

"Harry used to read to me. He always brought a book with him. Usually something he'd seen you reading. He'd read it to me every night and, after he left, I'd finish it. You have good taste, maybe a little hoity-toity."

I shut the door behind me, thinking that maybe this was how she kept Harry coming back all those years. She never gave him a choice.

AS SOON AS I GOT home I had a little session of contagious gagging over my own toilet. Then I took a shower, grateful for the endless supply of scalding water in New York apartments. I didn't want to go to the workshop, but I forced myself to get dressed and go. When I came in, Juliette was reading aloud a comic story about sanitary napkins.

Jackson blinked his near-albino eyelashes at me. "Have you got something new for us, Cleo?"

"Nothing," I said.

He came home with me. I needed to get our clothes off and go straight to bed, but all I wanted to do was hold him.

At two in the morning I finally told him what had happened. "The woman takes it for granted that I'm going to help her," I said. "As if having cancer erases what she did."

"No, it doesn't. But it's still awful."

"She never had an attractive personality, I can tell. God knows what this says about my dead husband. She's got a daughter in Portland who doesn't even like her. Damn Harry. It's like he wants to torture me some more."

He stroked my hair. "You're in turmoil. This isn't something you should know how to deal with."

"But she's the one with cancer," I said. "That's what it comes down to."

AT THE SUPERMARKET I BOUGHT a chicken, vegetables, strawberries, yogurt, chocolate, coffee, toilet paper, and a handful of purple asters, which I arranged in an empty pickle jar on the kitchen table. She held my arm as we walked to the naturopath, where I sat in the waiting room for almost an hour. While the chicken was roasting we played gin rummy, Tilly checking to make sure I counted the points correctly. We ate together while she told me, as if I might have been anybody, about dinners on the town with Harry, about the swanky place with the jazz band they went to every year for their "anniversary." It's possible my mouth hung open while I listened. I don't know what I might have said if she hadn't suddenly bent over from a bowel spasm.

The leftovers went into the fridge, the pots got washed

and herbal tea made. At the Strand I had bought a copy of *Larry's Party* because I knew that it was a novel about a decent, non-cheating man. Tilly said that Harry had done voices and accents but I read in a straight monotone. Still, she liked the book, at least until she fell asleep, breathing heavily, a line of drool dangling from the corner of her mouth.

It took me ten minutes to find a taxi in that part of Brooklyn at night. I was grateful to fall into the back seat, close my eyes, and feel myself moving away from that woman.

I COULD ONLY IGNORE THE filthy apartment for so long. I vacuumed the heavy curtains, beat the rugs on the little iron balcony, scrubbed the floors, the bathroom, the kitchen. I shampooed Tilly's wig and gave it a blow dry. All the time I gritted my teeth, sure that I would explode if she said even one thank you. But she never did, only suggested that I put new liners in the kitchen drawers.

We went by cab to the Cancer Center in Brooklyn Hospital, where the doctor talked to me as much as to Tilly, who wasn't taking a lot in. And that was how I spent a week, ten days, arriving in the late morning and staying until after dark. My apartment became a place to sleep. My brief bohemian life felt like something I'd read about in a novel.

For a few days I ignored Sarah's calls. When I finally answered she screamed at me long distance. "What exactly is going on? Tell me you didn't murder that woman."

"No such luck," I said. "Turns out she's left town. Won't be back for months. So I'm going to miss her."

"Good. Maybe now you can enjoy yourself. It would be nice if you called after school to say hi to the kids."

But I forgot to call. I was playing gin rummy and getting my ass kicked, as Tilly put it, having one of her more lucid moments.

I WASN'T WRITING ANY POEMS or making it to the workshop. Jackson and I met every second or third day for a meal, a late night drink, or just to lie sleepless in bed.

We were in an Indian restaurant on First Avenue. I said, "You have an old lady for a girlfriend, and not even much of her."

"I don't think this is doing you good," he said. "You look exhausted. You're not doing anything for yourself. And you're right. I'm not getting much of you."

I didn't have a smart reply or even a defensive one. I pushed the bangan bharta around on my plate.

TILLY GREW WEAKER. STRONGER PAINKILLERS made her more comfortable, but put her into a drowse. She leaned against my arm to get to the bathroom. She ate rice and Jello in bed.

Three nights in a row I fell asleep on the sofa and never made it home. On the third morning, waking in the same clothes, my skin feeling sticky and my mouth as if filled with porridge, I knew that Tilly would have to return to the hospital. She was still in her bedroom, presumably asleep. I picked up the telephone and called the daughter in Portland.

"Do you know what time it is here?" she said. "It's like five in the morning."

I couldn't have cared less. "When can you get here?"

A long pause. "If I can get a seat I should be in by eight or ten p.m. your time."

When I hung up I saw Tilly standing in the doorway, her nightgown unbuttoned. She said, "I made my own bed, I know. But I want to remember the good part. I want to remember Harry. Don't take that away from me."

It's the other way around, I thought. But all I said was, "Why don't we give you a bath. So you'll look nice when your daughter arrives."

We spent the day as usual. I made breakfast, lunch, and dinner, although she had almost stopped eating. We tried to play gin, but she couldn't concentrate. I read chapter after chapter of *Larry's Party*, not knowing how much she was taking in. She was in bed when I looked up from the book and saw that she was asleep, her tight mouth in a grimace.

I went into the living room and sat in an armchair. Eventually I, too, must have fallen asleep because I was roused by the sound of a key in the lock. Blinking, I saw the daughter come in with her small wheeled suitcase. She was maybe forty-five, with the same tulip-bulb nose as her mother.

"I phoned the hospital," I told her. "They know she's coming tomorrow."

I stood and picked up my bag. I thought to ask her why she hated her mother, whether it had anything to do with Harry. But I didn't have the energy. She brushed past me to the bedroom and I went out the door, closing it behind me.

It was late but I walked to the subway anyway. In the bright car, people were half-awake, probably on their way to night-shift jobs in the city. I got home, showered, put on new clothes, gathered up the ones I'd been wearing for three days and carried them down to the battered garbage bins under the porch outside. Then I walked around the corner and saw that Café Orlins where I used to go and write was still open. I took a table against the brick wall and ordered a coffee. I thought of calling Jackson, but decided to wait until tomorrow. Instead, I took my pen and notebook out and laid them on the table. I knew that I wouldn't write anything. I just wanted them there.

# Dreyfus in Wichita

MICHAEL SPEARMAN, MUSIC AND SCIENCE teacher of Beth Shalom Hebrew Day School, located in a former Toronto car dealership, was eating his leftover cold stir-fry when he read the following sentence:

> *As a demonstration of its sympathy for the disgraced French captain, Alfred Dreyfus, the citizens of Wichita, Kansas elected Miss Sadie Joseph, a Jewess, as its Carnival Queen for the year 1899.*

The book was a cultural history of nineteenth-century travel, of no use to the students of Beth Shalom, which only went up to grade nine; but, like many books in the school library, it had been donated in a carton of garage-sale leftovers. The basement — which housed the library, the science lab, the music room, and the furnace — had a fur of mildew growing between the cinder blocks. Down here, at least, Michael could think and dream and feel the quiet thrumming of disappointment in himself.

Reading the words again, he let the fork drop into the plastic tub. The thrumming became something else, grew louder, surged through his body, and roared into his ears. All he could do was stand up and begin to pace the room, manoeuvring around the battered music stands, the cellos abandoned on their sides. It was such a beautiful idea, what had come to him. Had he really found the subject through which he might finally release his dismally unused talent? For here, in this one sentence, was everything. A small town, in a period of tremendous change (the first motor cars, telephones, electric lights) and with brilliant period music to draw on. A story not of a great historic event itself, but of a small side-drama in a place far from the centres of power in which the largest themes might find expression. A heroine, hardly old or experienced enough to know herself, yet with intelligence and hidden resources, a girl on the verge of womanhood (with a marvellous soprano voice) who finds herself the absolute focus of attention of the town that is her world.

And what a great name! Sadie Joseph. So lovely in its ordinariness. The roaring in his head quieted just enough for the ideas to come pelting down. Sadie would be the daughter of the proprietor of the local dry-goods shop, the pivotal role around which circled equally important characters. The mayor looking for a way to survive a financial scandal. The idealistic Protestant schoolteacher who speaks of the Dreyfus case and so becomes the catalyst for the events. The president of the Honourable Men of Kansas

Society, Wichita chapter, with his racist grudge against Mr. Joseph and secret lust for Sadie herself. The young Jewish store clerk who is Sadie's unofficial fiancé and dismayed by her sudden celebrity. The mayor's son, decent and handsome, home from Harvard Law School, whose love for his father conflicts with his hatred of injustice. (Naturally he too must fall in love with Sadie). The jealous girl, who had previously been assured of the crown and the mayor's son for herself. The story would need somebody to tell it, an outsider, say a reporter from the big-city newspaper who arrives with a pen dripping cynicism but finds a chance at redemption for himself ...

So much came to Michael during that lunch break that he could hardly record it all in the copybook he pulled from his desk. When the afternoon class stormed down the basement stairs he was still scribbling frantically and did not even hear them.

MICHAEL HAD GROWN UP IN the eighties, witness to the death of punk, the rise of the pop superstars, MTV. He played in garage bands with his friends, thrashing their way through covers of early Elvis Costello and the Clash. But he continued his conservatory piano studies and in the school orchestra played the viola. He had to keep secret his fascination for Broadway musicals, sneaking out to see the bus-and-truck shows that came to the Royal Alexandra Theatre on King Street. At home he hunkered in the living room listening to his parents' collection of 33 1/3 RPM records: *Show Boat*, *Carousel*, *Annie Get Your Gun*, *Cabaret*.

His old garage-band friends went to work for law firms

or studied internal medicine or joined the family condominium-development company. Michael's music degree only got him a job at Sam the Record Man, so he went back for a year of teacher's college and spent nine months substitute teaching in the public school system before he got the job at Beth Shalom. He met a woman during the intermission of a local production of *Company*, a frizzy-haired animal-rights activist named Frida Yaffe who spoke French, Hebrew, and German, baked bread, and played clawhammer banjo. She disliked musicals but had won a free ticket while listening to CBC Radio. They lived together in her flat on Major Street and then bought the tiny house on Manning, near the cheap Korean restaurants. When tests finally revealed that her eggs were sterile, her melancholic nature deepened. Over the years they acquired two dogs, a cat, an African Grey Parrot, and a plastic bathtub of turtles, all of them rescued. The floorboards projected splinters into bare heels, the second-hand furniture wore out and was replaced by more second-hand furniture. They held on stubbornly to a certain idea of living, like ever-aging students.

MICHAEL WORKED ON THE SCORE, the lyrics, the book, when he could. Every holiday, including Yom Kippur, and of course the summer months. Over time he conceived a three-act structure and settled on the more traditional Broadway approach of a book with dramatic songs rather than the pseudo-operatic sung-through show. The first number had to be muscular but lyrical, a hymn to the sweetness of small town life that was about to be turned upside down. Then the narrative would start without delay with a scene of Sadie's boyfriend telling her she ought to enter this year's contest for Carnival Queen because she was the prettiest girl in town and the most talented, with her nightingale voice. Of course she would resist: "You forget, Nathan, what we are and how this town sees us," to which he would reply, "Ah, Saidie, that doesn't matter. Don't we have friends? Don't people like us? Doesn't the mayor himself shop at your father's store? It's almost the new century, Sadie. We're part of this place now. We belong here just like everybody else."

It was more work than he had ever imagined. Nine ballads, seven rhythm numbers, three specialty songs. Solving one structural problem caused three more to spring up — solos running back to back, characters acting against their motivations, the first-act curtain closer requiring too complicated a narrative set-up. If it hadn't been for Frida he might have given up. She would bring him a mind-stimulating herbal infusion and, kissing him on the neck, say, "Drink up, Wolfgang. Nobody said it was easy to be a genius." After a week or two, he would find another little revelation, a small breakthrough — the completion of a signature melody, the finding of a contrapuntal rhythm, a lyric that would say in five words what he'd been struggling to voice in pages of dramatic scene.

After eight months he could see the shape of the thing and, after another eight, some genuine dramatic moments and real musicality. It took a year to bring the rest up and ten months more of further discarding and ruthless revising. More polishing before he could score each of the orchestral parts — violins, violas, cellos, basses, the brass, woodwind, and percussion, and also mandolin, banjo, auto-harp, and mouth organ.

Michael was now forty-two. He felt relieved and humble, but also twitching with anxiety. Now that the work was done, what was he supposed to do with it? It had been easy to daydream in the basement of Beth Shalom Day School, but if there was one thing Michael knew about himself, it was that he had no entrepreneurial push.

Lying on their futon at night, Michael said into the dark, "What good is my musical if it never gets heard? It's just paper. But I don't seem to have the right kind of ambition. I want it to be performed — on Broadway, too. I just don't have the strength to do anything about it. Or even believe it could happen."

"You give up too easily," said Frida. Her frizzy hair had already begun to silver at the edges; she had map lines around her eyes. She'd grown thinner, too, and had been shocked by the onset of diabetes. "Do some research, Michael," she said. "Make a plan. You have to think of this as a direct action. Make some noise, sweetheart. Otherwise, nobody's going to hear your songs."

HE MUSTERED UP THE ENERGY to make a telephone call which, to his surprise, resulted in a meeting with David Mirvish in the office above the Royal Alexandra Theatre. Mr. Mirvish was attentive and sympathetic, but would not take the proffered copy of *Dreyfus in Wichita*. He spoke resignedly of the Canadian musicals that had failed — *Napoleon*, *Duddy!* — and told Michael that he would only consider his show if it was already a success like *The Drowsy Chaperone*.

Michael understood how this daydream had allowed him to believe that his life was more than the sum of its ordinary parts. He wished he'd never written the thing. When he opened the door he saw Frida standing in the tiny living room, one of the cats mewling against her ankles, holding a gift-wrapped present.

"Frida, why are you giving me something? I don't deserve it."

"*Sha*. You can be a pain in the ass, Michael. Just open it."

He unwrapped the large book carefully, knowing that Frida reused paper. *How to Sell Your Musical to Broadway and Make It Big*.

He turned it over. "You paid forty-two dollars for this?"

"You're welcome," she said and headed up the stairs.

THE BOOK LISTED THE NAMES of one hundred and seventy-three agents and fifty-six producers working on Broadway. Over the next two weeks Michael composed a cover letter, made copies of the score, bought mailing envelopes. The enterprise cost him just under three thousand dollars.

A week. Two. Four. "Well, of course," Frida said. She was knitting a shawl while stroking their blind dog with her toes. "There's an old-boy system at work. And look who they hire these days? Has-been rock stars. To write shows about superheroes. Something like *Dreyfus*, that finds relevance for our times, of course it's going to be a tough sell."

"Maybe the work's no good."

"It's good," she said.

"You don't even like musicals."

"That's right, and I like yours."

He noticed she was wearing her puff-sleeved top, with the lacing that criss-crossed the open bosom. She wore it when she wanted to have sex; she liked him to undo the lacing. But he felt no rise of desire. When she was looking down at her knitting he put his hand over his groin, to judge whether he might coax some life into the thing, so as not to disappoint her.

ARRIVING HOME THE NEXT DAY, he found Frida in the kitchen, adding beets to her vegetarian hotpot.

"There's a letter for you on the dining table."

"What do you mean a letter?" He was already moving through the doorway, picking up the envelope, reading the return address.

> *Cohn Musical Entertainment*
> *107 Fourteenth Street, Suite 3B*
> *New York, New York*
> *10375*

His hands started to tremble. Frida came up beside him, licking the wooden stirring spoon. "So? Open it."

Dear Mr. Spearman,

Dear? I ought to cry, Hail Spearman! For you are a true musical genius. Do you have any idea what your *Dreyfus in Wichita* means to a man like me? A producer can wait years, a whole lifetime even, and never make a discovery like this. Scores we get in the hundreds, thousands even. But to find one with such depth, such seriousness of intent, which manages nevertheless to entertain as it transforms its story into the idiom of the American musical — ah, how rare that is, Mr. Spearman, how rare!

Mr. Spearman — may I call you Michael? — I kiss your hands. Let me bring your masterpiece to the Broadway stage and the public it deserves. Please call me. Collect.

Yours in awe,
Mort Cohn, President

They danced, they laughed, they declaimed the letter aloud, first Frida and then Michael, and carried it triumphantly over their heads. After they had collapsed onto the afghan-covered sofa, Frida said breathlessly, "Go ... ahead ... and ... phone."

"Phone? Now?" The smile evaporated from Michael's face.

Frida just gave him a look. Then she reached to the end table and handed him the phone.

The other end picked up at the first ring. "Cohn Entertainment Group."

"Is Mr. Cohn available?"

"Who is calling?"

"Michael Spearman."

"Michael! I can't believe I am actually speaking to the composer of *Dreyfus in Wichita*. Let me assure you, I don't usually answer the phones around here, but the secretary's got strep throat. My God, you should see me — I've got tears in my eyes. I haven't cried like this since Lenny Bernstein died. Michael, listen to this —"

Michael heard the thin humming of Sadie's theme. Just as abruptly it stopped. "You hear, Michael? Already seared in my memory."

"Mr. Cohn, I'm amazed. I'm overwhelmed."

"As soon as I'm off the phone I'm going to talk to Hal and see how his schedule looks."

"Hal Prince? He's still working?"

"Hang on, Michael. Nancy, you're back. Start working on that Spearman contract. We'll FedEx it overnight. And make sure you get the names spelled right."

THE CONTRACT ARRIVED, NOT BY Federal Express, but regular mail. Along with the signature, it required a cheque for eight thousand dollars in U.S. funds. "Absolutely standard practice for a first-time composer," said Cohn himself, when Michael called. "Besides, read the whole clause. You become an investor in your own work. A percentage of the receipts goes to you, and not after we recoup but from *day one*. Everybody knows that Sondheim made almost nothing until he wised up. Do you want to be one of those shmucks who makes everybody rich except himself? You're a long term investment for me."

For three days Michael dithered, but he knew he would send the cheque. Frida refused to help him decide, but she looked sorrowful — "And not because of the money, honey," she said. He had to take out a loan against the equity in their house. Even as the envelope slipped into the mail box he knew it was gone forever. Shortly after he found Mort Cohn's phone to be disconnected, and mail sent to Fourteenth Street was returned "address unknown."

In June, Frida got arrested at the G20 protests and spent a night in jail. Michael was at home, sprawled on the sofa watching a DVD of *Rent* while absent-mindedly tossing grapes to the parrot. He didn't watch the news and so missed seeing Frida get dragged into a police van.

IN SEPTEMBER THE SCHOOL YEAR began, when most of the students had to be retaught the simplest fingerings of their instruments. He performed his teaching duties with grim conscientiousness.

"You know who I am in class?" he said to Frida. "I'm the guy in that Edvard Munch painting, *The Scream.*"

She was boiling pectin-free rhubarb jam in a cast-iron pot. "Boy, are your students lucky to have you."

"I don't care about my students anymore."

"Then you're in worse trouble than I thought," she said, stirring with the wooden spoon. "Maybe you ought to quit."

"We couldn't afford it."

"Yeah, well, your students can't afford you either. Now taste this and tell me if it's too tart. You must be good for something."

AS SOMETIMES HAPPENED, A NEW student enrolled in the school after the year had begun. Laura Appelbaum, a first-rate violinist, had started on the Suzuki method at the age of four. She took to visiting Michael in the music room at lunch hour so they could play duets. She had a natural ear, a fluid bow, an excessive love for the Romantics, pre-mature acne, a retainer, pigtails, and didn't seem to care about being considered a freak by her peers. At home, Frida became weirdly jealous listening to Michael go on about her, but she solved the matter by inviting Laura for dinner. The two hit it off instantly; they were, Michael could see, kindred spirits. They split their sides laughing over Laura's imitations of the Beth Shalom teachers, sparing only Michael himself because, as Laura put it, "You're not exactly the sort who can laugh at himself, are you, Mr. S.?"

For a month he held off telling Laura about his musical. Naturally, she asked to see the score. "I don't think so," Michael said gently. "I don't feel like disappointing you."

"Come on, Mr. S. I really, really want to see it. *Pweeze*?"

He sighed and pulled open the bottom drawer of his desk. She pulled it from his hands, gave it a friendly pat, and ran out of the music room.

Michael could not sleep because a twelve-year-old girl named Laura Appelbaum was reading *Dreyfus in Wichita*. He drove to school and sat in the music room limp with regret. It was three minutes to the bell when she slid through the doorway, the score under her arm.

"We've got to do it, Mr. S.!"

"Do it?"

"You know what I mean. It's great. It drags a little in the middle of the first act, and Sarah's ballad in act three is weak. But otherwise it's amazing. We can do it here at Beth Shalom. We've got the orchestra. Miss Litvak can direct and you can conduct. I'll be first violin, naturally."

"Wait, wait. This isn't a Garland and Rooney picture.

First of all, it's too musically sophisticated for kids. The syncopation, the minor keys, the harmonies —"

"Okay, so it's not *Grease*. But they'll get it. And if they get to skip some classes for rehearsals everybody will want to be in it. All we've really got to do is convince the principal."

"Yes, well, that ends it, doesn't it. Rabbi Pinkofsky won't possibly agree. He wants the school to concentrate on its academics and Jewish learning. He won't even give me a cent for new strings."

"Exactly. Which is why my Dad's idea is so good. He says that if we make the performance a fundraiser for the school, the Rabbi will go for it. Dad says —" she lowered her voice to a whisper "— there's asbestos under the ceiling tiles."

"I don't know, Laura."

"You're just like my little brother. You have to be asked ten times before you'll agree to something you want."

RABBI PINKOVSKY ASKED MICHAEL TO stand before his fellow teachers and give a synopsis of the work. He was saved only by the intervention of Ellen Litvak, who'd been dying to put on a musical for years. "In my view there's a real advantage in putting on Michael's show. Sure, we could do *Fiddler*, but we'd have to pay for the rights and that's not cheap. We don't have to pay Michael a dime."

In the end, the faculty voted in favour, with only the gym, mathematics, and *Halacha* teachers against. At home, Michael tortured himself over the decision. "My life's turning into a parody," he said to Frida.

"If you didn't want it you could have said no," Frida replied. "But I think you doth protest too much. You're secretly thrilled."

"Do I look thrilled?"

"You hide it. Disgust you'll show. Annoyance. Long-suffering weariness. Occasionally mild pleasure. But you never look thrilled, ecstatic, or blissful."

"Are you serious?"

"Oh yes, you can also look appalled, as now."

THE NEXT SEVERAL WEEKS FELT to Michael more like a caricature of the production process, a kid-sized version of *The Producers*. During the auditions he heard a dozen girls belt out "Somewhere Over the Rainbow" or songs by Lady Gaga, whoever that was. In the end he chose thirteen-year-old Shoshona Zeiss, who had taken singing and tap lessons. In the first rehearsals, Ellen Litvak had to simplify her choreographic ideas, especially for the boys who could hardly tell their right feet from their left. Michael held separate orchestra rehearsals in the basement, halting every two bars. At least he didn't have to worry about Laura's violin solos, or the banjo, which Frida would play. Shoshona projected sincerity, but was rather one-note and of course any underlying hint of sexual passion was lost entirely. The heavy boy cast as the mayor brought some energy but was a little too *Guys and Dolls*. Hardly their fault; they were modern kids, used to surfing internet porn and hearing lectures about STDs. They weren't mystified by the contradictory yearnings he had worked so hard to capture; they were simply unaware of them.

Michael arrived at school one morning to find the walls covered in posters.

WORLD PREMIERE!
ONE NIGHT ONLY!

Beth Shalom Day School presents

*DREYFUS IN WICHITA*

Book, Music, and Lyrics by Michael Spearman
Directed by Ellen Litvak

Saturday, December 21, 8 p.m.
Tickets $10. Available in Rabbi Pinkovsky's Office

Three days later, the posters had red banners pasted across them. SOLD OUT. Shoshona Zeiss and the other leads were strutting around like celebrities. Laura Appelbaum reported that the stage crew had taken to eating in the cafeteria only amongst themselves and that at least two actors were going to arrive on performance night in hired limousines. "O what hath thee wrought?" Frida teased, but it wasn't funny to him.

Rabbi Pinkofsky himself came down to the music room to offer his congratulations. Michael had always been nervous around the Rabbi, afraid (as he had been as a boy) to be asked a question or made to recite a passage from the Torah that he didn't know. "Mazel Tov," the rabbi said to Michael. "You've given us a new roof. Now it doesn't matter if it's a hit or a miss."

THE MORNING OF THE PERFORMANCE found Michael retching into the toilet. "Perfectly normal, honey," said Frida,
bringing him a wet cloth. "I hear Kauffman did it all the
time. Or was it Hart? Anyway, it brings good luck."

At school, Michael retched in the staff washroom while
Laura Appelbaum stood in the doorway with her violin case
under her arm. "You okay, Mr. S.?" she asked when he emerged,
pale and trembling. "You want me to get Mrs. Kofsky?"

"No, I'm all right now. There's nothing left inside me."

"The dry heaves, that's the worst. I can't wait for tonight!"

Somehow he held himself together through the teaching
day. At two o'clock an announcement over the P.A. called the
actors and crew from their classes for a final tech rehearsal.
A rented Klieg light fell, missing the big city reporter by
inches and causing Shoshona Zeiss to burst into tears. The
sets were taking an excruciatingly long time to change.

"I wanted *Peter Pan*," said Ellen Litvak, "and you've given
me *The Ring of the Nibelung*."

Back at the house, he lay on the sofa as if it were a berth
on the *S.S. Mauretania* in a heaving sea. What did he want
from it all? He hoped it wasn't a sick need for uncondi-
tional love, because he really didn't want it, he didn't want
anything from anybody or anybody to want anything from
him. He had, after all these years of teaching in a parochial
school, no prayer on his lips.

He woke to the touch of Frida's fingers caressing his
face. "Time to wake, Maestro," she said gently. "Come and
see what I've got you. Ta-da!"

It was a tuxedo. With tails. "Frida, I can't wear that. I'll
look ridiculous."

"Of course you can. Make the most of it, Michael. Embrace the moment."

She had to help him with the tie and cummerbund; she had to drive the Tercel up to school, her old Stella banjo rattling in the back seat. It was already dark when they arrived and a light snow was falling into the glow of lamps surrounding the former car dealership. In the first classroom they passed, mother-volunteers were powdering faces and applying rouge and eyeliner. Orchestra members were corralled in the teacher's lounge; they gave a ragged cheer when Michael and Frida entered. He set to work tuning the instruments.

Ralphie Neugeboran, headset on, looked into the room. "Okay, orchestra. Follow me."

"Show time," Laura said. She pulled Michael down by his tuxedo sleeve and gave him a quick kiss on the cheek. "Good luck, Mr. S." They filed down the hallway to the rear door of the cafeteria, where the lunch tables had been converted to benches. One of the flute players knocked over a music stand, but somebody else caught it. In the audience there was a jostling for the last seats. The lights dimmed. A spotlight came up on the conductor's stand and Michael began to walk up the aisle. The applause sounded muffled and far away. He reached the stand and had a sudden moment of panic over his baton, but there it was in the inside pocket. He smiled gratefully at Frida, who winked at him. Now Laura played her A string and the other instruments pretended to tune up. He held out his hand for silence. He raised the baton, took a deep breath, and cut the air for the first, discordant burst from the brass section.

THREE HOURS AND FIFTEEN MINUTES later, the baton came down for the last time, drawing a fading note from the first violin. On stage, frozen in their final poses against the background of the town square, were all the major characters: the mayor holding back his anguished son, the father clutching his heart, the jealous girl with her hands clenched as if in supplication to a higher power, the newspaper man with his notepad discarded at his feet; and young Sadie Joseph, collapsed in the arms of her fiancé, hair trailing down, eyes closed, face bloodless. The only figures moving were a ghostly chain of bearded men in hats and long, dark coats, and women in kerchiefs and shawls, prefigurations of the larger tragedy to come. They had been Ellen's idea and he had argued against them, but their appearance had drawn gasps from the audience.

The stage went dark. He looked down at his exhausted musicians. Laura Appelbaum was visibly panting, her face glistening with perspiration. The applause had already begun. He turned to the audience — the fathers rising stiffly, the children sprawled asleep in their mothers' arms — before turning back again. Only now did he look to Frida with her banjo, chagrined that he had not sought her out first, but she was smiling up at him, her eyes shining. He could not keep his eyes on her and looked upwards towards the temporary grid of lights, feeling so bereft that he wondered if somebody close to him had died, somebody he could not at this moment remember. There were whistles and cheers in the audience, as if they were at a ball game. He felt hungry and thought with a wolfish anticipation of the boxes of limp Kosher pizza and cans of ginger ale. His gaze descended to the actors bowing, standing in a row and holding hands, children again. Shoshona was motioning to the orchestra and for some reason to him. The applause swelled. He turned and smiled, touched his finger to his brow, and remembered who had died.

# Lost at Sea

AT SIX IN THE MORNING, the first Sunday of June, 1979, he stood with his suitcase at the corner of Bayview Avenue and York Mills Road. There was no traffic: the one car climbing the hill he recognized by the red and yellow panels and the painted rectangle obscuring the name of the former taxi company. She pulled over. He tossed his suitcase into the trunk and got in.

He kissed her. "I picked up coffee and muffins," she said, smiling as she pulled out again, towards the ramp to the 401.

"What time did you get up?" he asked.

"I couldn't sleep. You know, I could have picked you up at your house. I wouldn't have come in."

"Please, Nadia, don't start."

"I'm not, really. I can't believe we're on the road. Can you find that oldies station on the radio? I want to sing in a very loud and out-of-tune voice."

"You got it," he said and relaxed.

They were both twenty-three, both recent graduates
from the University of Toronto. He was going to do an M.A.
in political science, but would probably end up in business
or law. She had been a scholarship student in French, but
had surprised and vaguely disappointed him by applying to
a chiropractic college in Ottawa. She was still undecided.
He understood that she might be hurt by his not introduc-
ing her to his parents. But her family was Ukrainian. During
the war, Ukrainian peasants had murdered his mother's
aunt and uncle and their three children, who had been
hiding in the woods. It wouldn't matter to his parents
that Nadia's family had been educated leftists living in
Odessa. Nadia's father had been a journalist, her mother
a high-school history teacher. After arriving in Toronto in
the late fifties she had raised the children while he had
begun a new career — driving a cab. Lively, engaged people,
they had welcomed Jeffrey into their small house in the east
end. Surely, he thought, Nadia could understand the difficult and unflattering position he was in.

They took a washroom break outside Rochester, stopped
for lunch at a roadside diner, and pressed on into the
afternoon. He missed an exit while she was napping and
had to wake her up so she could help him double back. For
dinner, they pulled up at a café just over the Massachusetts
border. They ordered a hamburger for him, a Greek salad
for her, and more coffee. Jeffrey stretched out his cramped
legs under the table. He looked at Nadia, her pale blue
eyes, her thin lips and fine bangs. Hours of driving and she
still looked exhilarated to be away from her tedious summer
office job.

There was something that he hadn't told her and couldn't tell her, not now when she was so simply and purely happy to be going somewhere new. He felt almost nauseated, but he pushed it as far down as he could — for her sake, he believed, even more than his.

She drove the last long stretch, the evening sun shifting from the back to the driver's side window as they rode up the curve of Cape Cod. There was ocean on either side of them though all they saw in the dusk were scrub trees filling the long gaps between the towns. Nadia turned the overhead light on and, juggling the map in her lap, said that she wanted to stop somewhere before they got to where they were staying. Each house, clapboard and shingle, had a wooden porch with maybe a bathing suit draped over the rail or some float boards piled up or a couple of glasses and a bottle of wine. Then the roads got narrower and the houses farther apart. They reached a dead end with a modest widening to allow room for ten or fifteen parked cars. Theirs was the only one. Nadia turned off the ignition, raised her eyebrows mischievously, and got out.

The air was sharp with the taste of salt and seaweed. Beyond a leaning fence was a grassy rise. When they got to the crest he saw the endless beach curving away from the ocean.

"How did you know to come here?" he asked.

"It helps to read the guidebooks."

She pulled him along to a stairway of greying cedar boards zigzagging down. "Cornhill Beach," she called it. They walked through tufts of grass until it was all sand. He could not quite take in how far the beach stretched or that it was deserted, despite all the footprints. He scooped up a handful of sand that was more like tiny stones the colour of quartz. They took off their shoes and he felt a pleasant pricking on the soles of his feet.

Closer to the water, the stones being larger, his feet almost hurt. The water's edge was marked with pale-brown foam, while a few inches higher lay dried seaweed, an inky line running for miles. The submerged stones had turned green with algae. He stepped into the water. Nadia told him that they were actually facing the bay and that the water on the other side of the cape, on the open ocean, was even colder.

He reached out to take her hand.

BACK IN THE CAR, DRIVING, they got lost. He peered through the windshield into the dark, blinking away fatigue and forcing himself not to go into a ditch. Nadia was relying on her hand-written instructions, which did not seem to match the roads. "Here! Turn right!" she cried out. He turned the wheel sharply, evergreen branches scraping the side of the car, and saw the ochre glow of a porch light ahead.

The house was larger than most of the others they had passed, but it too had a face of painted boards and cedar shingle sides. He already knew from Nadia that the main part of the house was over two hundred years old. By the time they pulled their suitcases from the trunk, there was a woman waiting for them in the light under the door. A large woman wearing a peasant dress and a heavy amber necklace. As they came up, she said, "Poor things, you must be exhausted." Two miniature dachshunds nipped at their ankles.

"I've been expecting you the last hour. Such a long drive from Canada! Just put your bags down anywhere, we'll worry about them later. The dogs don't really bite, they just need to get to know you. Leo! Theo! Stop being such bad children. Theo's actually a girl. Please, come and sit down. This is your house, too."

The woman's name was Toni with an "i"; she still had her Dutch accent. A wide, smiling face, very round eyes surrounded by many lines, hair cut short and close. Inside were high ceilings, dark wooden beams, wide-plank pine floors, and furniture that was handsome and solid. A low bookcase separated the modern and open kitchen from the long living room. On the walls were horizontal unframed paintings that Jeffrey guessed were Toni's, landscapes of beaches and an ocean so pale they faded away.

The three of them sat at the farm table before a fresh-baked loaf of bread, some cheeses, a bowl of fruit, and another of nuts and dried apricots. The dogs were impossible for him to tell apart, although Nadia was calling each by name and scratching it between the ears. The kettle whistled. Toni poured boiling water into a Chinese teapot.

"Are you both going to study with Bernie?" Toni asked, hovering with the teapot.

"No, no," he said. "Only Nadia. She's the one who's good with her hands."

"Oh, you must be good with your hands for some things, yes?"

He was too startled by the good-natured leer to reply. Nadia said quickly, "He's good enough for me." She pointed at a chair by the stone fireplace. "Is that one of Bernard's?"

A high-backed Windsor chair, carved seat, finely turned legs, comb-like back of delicate-looking spindles. The spindles went through a curving piece whose ends became the armrests, carved to look like the paws of a cat. It was painted a pale blue, faded where it was most rubbed so that the wood shone underneath. At first, the chair had been just a part of the furnishings of the room; it didn't call attention to itself. but looked at directly, it displayed a quiet beauty.

He watched as Nadia knelt in front of it, running her hands over the wood. Then she stood and lowered herself into the chair. And smiled. "It's so comfortable. Come try it, Jeffrey."

She gave up her place. He too couldn't help smiling.

"I want one," he said.

"I'm going to build you one."

"Oh, sure. Then you'll keep it for yourself."

"Nope, the first one's yours."

"You are a lucky boy," said Toni.


THEY DIDN'T WAKE UNTIL ALMOST eight, the light streaming through the uncurtained windows. They took a shower together, lathering each other's hair. Downstairs, Toni had left a note saying that she and the dogs had gone sketching. *Just put the espresso pot on the stove. Eggs, cheese, bread in the fridge. Cereals on the counter. Take what you like. Love, Toni.* On the table were a pot of flowers and a basket of freshly baked muffins. Also a pile of local newspapers, which they read aloud to one another as they ate: a man charged with stealing a crate of cranberries, a municipal debate on allowing nude bathing on another beach. Nadia was distracted — anxious, he thought, about her first morning. But he also knew that she didn't like to speak directly about how she felt, as if she had learned as a child not to show weakness or need.

Until two weeks ago, he hadn't known that Nadia was even considering anything other than chiropractic college. His earlier reaction to her decision about becoming a chiropractor had clearly upset her; she had felt obliged to explain that helping people to feel better would suit her. Besides, seeing her father drive and her mother give up work altogether had made her crave more security. The hours were flexible, she could work part-time if she wanted, even out of her home.

All that had made sense, but it still seemed like a waste to him. And then at the beginning of May she had told him, as carelessly as could be, that she wanted to go to Cape Cod and spend one week apprenticing to a furniture maker named Bernard Aronson. She had read an article in *The New York Times* about how he used only traditional hand tools to make reproductions of early Americana. It was physical work, too, another kind of usefulness, and she had long had a fantasy of working as an artisan of some kind. So she had telephoned him out of the blue. And, when Bernard Aronson invited her to come, she decided that, before committing herself to the chiropractic college, she ought to consider doing something she might not merely like but love.

This idea appealed to him much more; Nadia in some old-fashioned workshop, sawdust in her hair, working steadily while classical music played on the radio. He knew she wanted something from him, some sign about how he saw

the future. But he didn't feel he had a right to influence her
one way or the other. He merely said that it sounded like
something she might like and that it could be a great holiday
if he came with her. Her response was to throw her arms
wildly around him.

Bernard Aronson's house was in Wellfleet, only a few
minutes away on the bay side. Jeffrey drove along Main
Street, past cafés, antique shops, and wooden-fronted galleries. Nadia directed him down Pole Dike Road, through a
small wood, to the house. It was cedar-shingled, square,
with a stone chimney. A wooden sign hung from a wrought-
iron stand in the unruly front garden: *Aronson Period
Furniture*.

Nadia hesitated at the door, perhaps, he thought, to
savour a moment that, for all she knew, would change her
life. When she knocked, a voice sounded behind the door
which was then opened by a woman, very short, with dishev-
elled grey hair and black glasses, in robe and slippers.

"I can do something for you?" A strong New York accent.

"I'm Nadia. I'm supposed to apprentice with Bernard
Aronson."

"Of course. How did I forget?" The woman made as if
to slap herself on the forehead. She called over her shoulder, "Bernie, get your lazy ass out of bed! The girl is here!"
And then to Nadia and Jeffrey, "Come in, please. I'm Sadie,
wife of the genius. We were up late last night. Some friends
came over with their homemade wine. Give me a little
squeeze, darling. We're going to be friends. And who is the
young man with you?"

"My boyfriend, Jeffrey."

"Handsome. But those dark eyes, hmm. You want some coffee? Where are you staying?"

"We've had some already," Nadia said. "We're staying at Toni's."

"Is she waiting to hear from that son of hers? She's always waiting. It can't hurt to have another cup. Bernie! Put your pants on already. You're making a bad impression."

The rooms were small. They went through a dark vestibule into the kitchen, crockery arranged on open shelves, cast-iron pots hanging, percolator on the stove. "So you're from Canada?" she said. "I don't know what you said to convince Bernie to take you on. He doesn't usually like people around while he's working. He's an antisocial bear."

"She can be very persuasive," Jeffrey said.

"Oh yes, I see that," Sadie said. "You seem quiet, honey, but you know just what you want. Look, here comes the master now. It's about time."

Bernard Aronson came into the kitchen from the other side. He was equally short, squat and powerful-looking, with a large face, thick features, and curly hair that looked like a wig. "Sadie, why are you boring these people to death? You must be Nadia. Pleased to meet you." He shook both their hands, his grip almost painfully strong.

His wife said, "You need something to eat, Bernie. I'll make you eggs."

He brushed her off with a wave and picked up a bun, which he tore a bite out of. "Just give me coffee. Nadia hasn't come this far to watch me eat overcooked eggs. She wants to build a chair."

"As if there aren't enough chairs in the world."

"Sure, if you like sitting on junk." He smiled at us. "We'll go into the shop and take the grand tour."

"Me he doesn't even allow in."

"You are a busybody. Aren't you going in to work?"

"I have a late start." To them she said, "I work in a dentist's office over in Orleans. Somebody needs to bring in a regular paycheque."

Bernie ignored her. "We'll go out back."

They followed him out the door and around the house. There were five wood piles and boards in several lengths. "We're going to start over there," he said, pointing to some logs. "We're going to rive the legs and spindles out of a log — split them off, basically. The wood will be nice and green. It's a good way to get your frustrations out."

At the rear of the property, just before a line of trees, was the workshop, also cedar-shingled, with square windows; not old, but built to match the house. The door wasn't locked. Bernie turned on the lights, catching the wood dust in the air. There were work benches along the sides, rows of wooden-handled tools, antique lathes, various saws and vices, piles of cans. Near the back, several pieces looked nearly finished: a large armoire, a small, delicate-legged desk.

"This is so great," Nadia said.

"Nice to hear somebody else say it. You kind of take it for granted after a few years. So, Nadia, I think you should build what's called a sack-back chair. They're real nice."

"And we can actually do it in a week?"

"Oh sure. If you don't go running off to the beach every afternoon. But, before we do anything else, we're going to have a lesson on safety. So this doesn't happen to you."

He held up his left hand; half the pinky finger was missing. "Then we're going to get familiar with wood. Eastern white pine. Sugar pine. Yellow poplar, basswood, red and white birch. Red oak, hickory, white ash. I hate to ask, but did you bring the apprentice fee?"

"Yes, of course," Nadia said. She fumbled in her knapsack and pulled out a thick envelope of bills. Jeffrey hadn't heard about any fee. Bernie took the envelope and tossed it onto the workbench.

"All right, then. Let's get started. We'll be done by four o'clock, Jeffrey. I think Nadia will have had enough for the first day."

The man was telling him to take off. "Right," Jeffrey said. "I'll pick you up at four, Nadia." Nadia gave him a kiss. Her face glowed with pure happiness. They were already moving to a bench as he left the workshop.

AT THE HOUSE, TONI LENT him a girl's bicycle and he rode it back to Wellfleet. He went into the hundred-and-fifty-year-old hardware store, looked at the dories turned into flower boxes and set along the sidewalks, gazed up at the First Congregational Church with the clock in its steeple and a bell that rang on ship's time. He found a used bookstore, a little corner place with racks of paperbacks and piles of old sailing magazines. On a low shelf were seven copies of *Moby-Dick*. He chose a small, thick hardcover with woodcuts by Rockwell Kent. It had an inscription inside: *To Mattie who has harpooned my heart Christmas 1959.*

He went into a café for lunch and began to read the novel. But soon he had to stop. An increasing agitation came over him and he felt an unbearable panic, his heart thrashing in his chest.

*Don't*, he said to himself, *just don't*. He needed to be here and nowhere else. Slowly his heart subsided.

He rode to the nearest beach. People were swimming, laughing, and splashing each other. Little kids with sand on their bellies carried buckets. Shoes in hand, he walked in the cold water. Then he lay down in the afternoon sun and read *Moby-Dick*. When it was time, he rode back to the house, got the car, and drove to pick up Nadia, desperately impatient to see her.

IT WAS NADIA WHO recognized the man in the photographs on a side table. "Didn't we see him in a movie?" she said.

Jeffrey recognized him, too; a Hollywood actor who usually played the estranged son or the boyfriend cheating on the heroine. Or else the rich snob who gets what he deserves. Because of something a little sinister in his good looks. At breakfast, Toni confirmed that he was her son, the "wonderful boy" who often said he was going to visit but rarely made it. "He's supposed to come any time. He's shooting some television miniseries in Boston. But those shoots are awful, they keep the actors working day and night."

Driving to the workshop, Jeffrey said that it felt surreal to speak of someone they'd seen only on screen as if he were an ordinary person. "This is Cape Cod," Nadia said. "Everyone here knows somebody famous."

EVERY DAY HE GOT ON the bike. He saw the handsome houses in Brewster that had been built by wealthy sea captains, the lighthouse at Chatham, the Marconi wireless station. He watched boats unloading oysters. He walked along beaches that touched the ocean or Nantucket Sound or Cape Cod Bay. He read *Moby-Dick*, which so belonged to this place and the surrounding sea that he was sure he'd never be able to separate the memory of them.

And every day he waited with an intense desire for the time when he could pick up Nadia. Sometimes he went a half hour early, to see her work. He watched her sculpt the seat with a tool called a gutter adze, which looked like a short pick-axe with a curving blade. He watched her turning one of the legs on the lathe while pointing out to him the various carved elements by their names: wafer, vase, ring, neck. He came even earlier one afternoon to watch her steam and bend the top of the chair back.

She was always hot and tired, fine wood dust clinging to her sweaty skin. He brought bathing suits and towels and they would drive to Longneck Beach, on the ocean side. Holding hands, they ran screaming into the water. The cold was a delirious punch knocking the breath out of him.

BERNIE TOLD HER TO take a day off. They drove up to Provincetown where, while having breakfast in a Portuguese bakery on Commercial Street, he first saw two men kiss. On the wharf they bought tickets for a battered boat called the *Ranger*. There were about twenty passengers already aboard. The captain, a young man with an earring, used a microphone to tell them about the ocean environment and the history of whaling. But he became quiet for long stretches and they had nothing to do but look out at the endless water. With the engines cut, they drifted in the waves. The surface broke and two grey-blue forms leapt up, their bodies twisting in the air. Humpbacks. Disappearing for a minute or two, they rose again calmly, blowing fine spray. Then they dove, leaving two spots, exactly their shape, on the surface.

Jeffrey drove home in the dark, Nadia leaning sleepily against him. They slipped into the house, he leading, and crept up to their bedroom. Slowly undressing her, he kissed her mouth, her arms, her breasts, her belly, her cunt. She pulled him towards her. The headboard began to thump against the wall; they'd forgotten again to pull the bed away.

She pushed him over, put herself on top, sat almost upright, making small squeals with each forward motion. He tried to keep his mind clear, to think only of her. Lightning suddenly turned the windows silver; thunder shook the room. They heard the downpour, a battering on the roof above. They pulled away from one another and Nadia led him to the window where they stood naked, watching the storm. He had never seen one so violent.

The storm subsiding, they finished their lovemaking, and soon were sleep.


ANOTHER SPECIAL TOOL NADIA USED reamed the sockets for the legs, tapering them to fit snugly. The legs needed to splay out at the proper angle. The strength and durability of the chair depended on a web of tensions holding everything firm.

AFTER THEIR LATE AFTERNOON SWIMS, they would go to a
restaurant in Wellfleet or another nearby town and eat
crabs, or scallops, or big bowls of chowder. Towards the
end of the week Toni conveyed a dinner invitation from
her friends Mona and Lucy, who managed a gallery in
Provincetown where she showed her work. They owned a
small but perfect Cape house with a postcard view of the
ocean. The other guests were artists and writers who lived
nearby. They expressed pleasure at having "young people"
in their company. A giant pot was boiling on the stove,
ready to accept the lobsters. On the long table were corn
on the cob, heaps of coleslaw, and many bottles of wine.
The talk was loud and punctuated by shrieks of laughter.
Nadia spoke to a man who made sculptures out of objects
found on the beach; Jeffrey talked to a woman who did
pen-and-ink drawings of shells and seagulls and children's
toys left in the sand. Every few months she bundled up a
package of them and put them in the mail to *The New Yorker*.
The editor chose four or five to use as spot drawings, break-
ing up the columns of type. "They always choose the worst
ones."

Toni got notably drunk and began to sing in Dutch. At
two in the morning they helped her to the car. Jeffrey didn't
know how to drive stick-shift, so Nadia took them home
along the backroads. As they pulled up to the house, they
saw a convertible parked at the side. Someone was sitting
in a porch chair with a beer in his hand. When he stood
up, Jeffrey recognized him as the son in all the photographs.

Toni opened the jeep door and fell out. She climbed
onto the porch and put her big arms around her son. He

had a winning laugh and was, if anything, better-looking in person than in the movies.

Jeffrey himself had drunk too much and felt the bed swim beneath him. Sometimes the voices of Toni and her son drifted upstairs. She sounded as if she might be crying. Nadia curled herself around him and he closed his eyes.

In the morning, the convertible was already gone. Toni did not come down for breakfast.

IT TOOK NADIA AN ENTIRE day to assemble the sack-back: inserting the arm posts, drilling the sockets for the narrow spindles that would fan out to form the back, getting the stresses to play against one another. Now it was a true chair, the parts forming an elegant whole yet still marked with the signs of handwork. The next day, she wet the wood to raise the grain for the final laborious sanding, followed by the traditional method of painting with a mixture of white lead, turpentine, linseed oil, and pigment. It did not have the thickness of modern paint and the mustard colour was pleasingly uneven. Over time, Bernie said, the rubbing of arms and rear-ends would bring out more subtleties.

SHE HAD THE AFTERNOON OFF while the paint dried. They drove through shady towns until they began to pass the motels and fast-food stops that marked the entrance to Hyannis. Continuing straight to the dock, they parked the car to board the ferry.

The ride would take a couple of hours, the ferry swaying gently in the choppy water. On the deck they drank coffee and read their books. Despite the secure feeling of the wide ferry, he felt rising in him an unaccountable fear of drowning. It became hard to breathe. There came to mind a moment long forgotten, when as a child he had walked far out onto the sand of a Florida beach and been caught by a fast incoming tide. He had tried to struggle back through the waves, but they kept pushing him off his feet, forcing water into his mouth. Struggling harder, head plunging again below the surface, he knew that he was going to die. And then he felt his mother's strong arms around him.

Nantucket Island hove into view. He and Nadia and the other floppy-hatted, camera-toting tourists were disgorged into the village. Cobblestone streets, white-plank churches; it was almost too charming. Nadia took his arm and steered them away from the crowds. After only a couple of blocks they found themselves alone. She began to tell him how much she had learned over the week, not just the specific tasks needed but a whole approach, a way of thinking about work and life.

He said, "So what are you going to do? Is there some technical college for woodworking you can go to? Or a furniture maker back home for a longer apprenticeship?"

"I'm not going to do anything. I mean, I'm going to go to chiropractic college."

"Why?"

"Because it's a dream. Bernie is respected, even famous in his field. But he still can't make enough to properly support himself. If Sadie hadn't come into some family money, they never would have survived. He's got no pension, a crappy health insurance plan. I know that the romance would wear off. Maybe in two years, maybe in five. Bernie told me that, too. He says he's glad that I came, to remind him why he wanted to do this in the first place. Jeffrey, I want a house one day. I want to have kids. There's so much that I can learn from this week, I don't regret a moment of it. Even if it's the only chair I ever make. Ah, you look so disappointed. It really is okay. It's more than that. I feel great — about everything. Hey, look."

Pulling him close, she led them through the tilting, wrought-iron gate of a small cemetery. In the tall grass stood rows of thin headstones, white and flaking. He both tried and refused to understand what she was feeling, even as he looked at the simple carvings in the stone — a skull, a cross, a willow tree. The word *Sailor* was chiselled after some of the names and underneath, *Lost at Sea*.

Nadia turned to face him. "It's good luck to kiss in a cemetery," she said, grabbing the sleeves of his jacket.

"And where did you hear that?"

"I'm sure that I read it in a guidebook," she whispered.

ALL THAT WAS LEFT WAS the final rubbing with boiled linseed oil. The chair was done.

Jeffrey came for a celebratory lunch in the back garden beside Sadie's vegetable patch. Bernie opened a bottle of "good old American champagne." They raised their glasses to the beautiful chair, which rested nearby on the grass. They ate quiche and salad, and Nadia, who didn't feel comfortable being the centre of attention, asked Sadie about her childhood.

"My father was a cantor at the Brooklyn Beth David Synagogue. He had a beautiful voice. But it made him too full of himself. Women were drawn to him. He ran off with a member of the choir when I was twelve. Years later, he tried to contact me but what he did to my mother I could never forgive. Now Bernie and me, we met at a sing-a-long in Washington Square Park. June 1949. His father wanted him to be a pharmacist, but Bernie had these back-to-the-land ideas. We rented a farm in Upper New York State. Some farmhouse, huh, Bernie? It was falling down. That's when you started building furniture. Thank God, because you were no farmer."

"And you were no farmer's wife," he said.

"But enough," she said, raising a second glass. "A toast to Nadia and her chair."

"I can't even begin to thank you both."

"You have learned much, grasshopper," Bernie said, raising his own glass. "As we like to say on the Cape, *L'chaim!*"

FOR THEIR LAST AFTERNOON THEY went to a freshwater lake off Calhoon Hollow Road. The water was warm and the bottom soft sand. They played like kids in the shallows, chasing and splashing one another. For dinner they went to a shack in Wellfleet and sat on outdoor benches, eating from baskets of fried fish and drinking beer. Afterwards they went for a walk, drove home, packed, and got ready for bed early. When he came out of the bathroom, Nadia was already asleep.

THEIR TRAVEL ALARM RANG AT six. They had a quick breakfast. Toni gave them smothering hugs. At Bernie's, they wrapped the chair in groundsheets and tied it to the roof of the car with a foam slab underneath. Bernie and Sadie, squat as a couple of Hobbits, waved as they pulled away.

Traffic was light and before long they were off the Cape. But the rest of the drive felt long and wearying. They kept the radio on the entire way, switching to the CBC close to the border. It was late as they drove along the 401 past the first exits to Toronto. His eyes wanted to close; cars ahead seemed to blur and double. Suddenly his hands started to tremble. At the Bayview exit he took the ramp into the empty suburban streets. Slowly he drove past cul-de-sacs and crescents until he pulled into his parents' driveway.

He turned off the ignition.

"We did it," she said and yawned.

"I'm exhausted. But it was a great trip. Really amazing."

"I'll see you tomorrow?"

"Sure. Let's have coffee. I need to talk about something."

"What do you need to talk about?" she asked.

"Tomorrow's better," he said lightly.

She kept looking at him. "No," she said. "Tell me now. Please."

"I don't want to tell you now."

"You have to."

His breathing was shallow. He felt almost faint. "I think we have to stop seeing each other."

"What does that mean?"

"I'm sorry, I'm really sorry."

"You can't just do that, Jeffrey. You have to tell me why."

"I'm trying to do the right thing."

"You have to tell me."

"Nadia, I met somebody."

"You met somebody? When?"

"Two weeks ago."

"You went out with her? You slept with her?"

"No, no. I just met her, that's all. At that birthday thing I went to for my cousin."

"But we've been going out for a year. We just spent a week together."

"I know. And it was great. I mean it. I couldn't say anything before — I didn't want to spoil it."

They sat there in the dark.

"How do you know if you're right about something," he said, but not as a question.

She got out of the car. By the time he came around she had pulled his suitcase from the back seat. Then she stood on the door rim and reached up to cut the ropes with a pocket knife. Tears streamed down her face but she kept cutting. He said, "Don't, Nadia. Please don't," but she kept moving around the car and before the last ropes were cut the chair began to slide. She eased it down to the drive and pulled off the groundsheets.

She reached into the car and flung out his *Moby-Dick*.

"I didn't know what to do," he said.

"Please don't phone me. Or contact me in any way. I really mean it." She closed the knife and put it in the glove compartment, shut the passenger door, went around to the other side and got in.

She backed up quickly, swung around in the road, and drove off.

He stood there a long time, surrounded by the ground-sheets and pieces of rope. Finally he carried the chair into the garage.

THE CHAIR IS NOW OVER thirty years old.

Both his children slept in his arms as newborns in it, his daughter and then his younger son. When the daughter was in graduate school and the son was taking a year to travel, his marriage ended and he moved into a condominium with an extra bedroom for whichever child might wish to stay.

He placed the chair in the small living room by the bay window. Every day he sits there and reads. Bernie Aronson was right. With use, the paint and wood has become worn and smooth. Age has made it more beautiful.

# The Little Underworld of Edison Wiese

EDISON THINKS:

*How terrible is the morning rush, so many desperate faces, such weighty grief. And always we fail in our modest but honourable responsibilities.*

Take it as evidence of Edison's delusions, this fragment of the unrolling inner monologue. Edison fills a line of Styrofoam cups with boiled coffee, lids and then nestles them into paper bags beside muffins, croissants, bagels with slabs masquerading as cream cheese. He takes in bills, he gives change. It is the usual morning crush, if perhaps a bit more frantic owing to this being the last day of the year, and Edison's thoughts would have to be considered exaggerated by any balanced person. Perhaps it is a good thing that he cannot get these thoughts out easily, for Edison stutters, an impediment since early childhood. Already he is on his third carafe of the morning and has to turn from the counter to fill a new filter with grounds. As the morning customers all want American coffee, the espresso machine sits *forlorn* (Edison's word) on the adjacent counter, its brass dome reflecting the *gaunt visages* (Edison again) as they swarm and recede. Many of those customers are already pulling back the plastic tabs to take scalding swallows before they are even out of the café.

*And this is how we should live out our days? Without comfort or consolation, or love, or even the pleasure of stillness? If only I, even in so humble a profession, could make their pain ease a little. But hardly do I have time to say "Good morning" before they are gone again. Am I not here to serve them in some more profound manner?*

Yes, it is undoubtedly fortunate that the customers cannot hear, for a person simply does not have such thoughts in the café of an underground mall, with a sixty-three-storey building overhead. Several cellphones begin to chime at the same moment; hands reach into jackets, purses, briefcases. *To be an oasis in a desert of despair!* Edison moans inwardly, reaching for packets of Sweet 'N Low. *And each one of you a Job, proving — or disproving — His existence by your own trials.*

THE WASP MAKES HER WAY to the counter. He calls her this because of the tightly fitted belt — a device for self-suffocation — that the tiny woman wears banded round the waist of her dress. Her face, though, is large and tragic: pale as flour, with eyes and mouth painted to affect an artificial brightness. This morning her lipstick is smudged at one corner; how Edison longs to fix it with a napkin. The Wasp puts down exact change, picks up her coffee without a word, and wobbles away on impossible heels.

*It's the women I feel most sorry for. Does that make me a senti-mentalist? How they look like corpses in the morning. And who knows what fears are a burden to their thoughts? Is a child home with fever? Are their husbands brutal or indifferent? Do they yearn for the strong hand, the warm touch in an empty bed? Such unhealthy, unreadable faces.*

Already her place is taken by a man with a caterpillar moustache, bellowing his order. *I am not deaf, sir, not deaf.* The clock behind the counter shows a quarter to nine, the worst fifteen minutes of the day. Edison turns, pours, bags, punches the register. *I am not a waiter but an automaton.* If only Beatrice would help, but he knows she is already pressed to the phone in the back room, her world crumbling. So Edison works alone to keep the horrors at bay.

But wait. You need to know how Edison got here. How he became a waiter in a café under the ground, in the *heartless heart of the city.* Then you will see how ridiculous he is.

EVERY WEEKDAY EVENING, FOR THE past two-and-a-half months, Edison has set his alarm clock for five-thirty. He goes to sleep at nine, the same bedtime he knew as a child. He still closes the door on the same room, surrounded by his globe, his *World Book Encyclopedia,* his collection of miniature flags of the United Nations. He still lies on the same bed, looks at the wallpaper of dancers in traditional ethnic costumes as he grows drowsy.

"W-w-one day," Edison used to tell his mother and father, "I'm g-going to visit every great city in the world." He had learned the names of each of those cities by the age of twelve yet now, at thirty-three, he has been nowhere but Niagara Falls and Miami Beach. For all his dreaming, Edison is terrified of going anywhere.

When he was in his mid-twenties, Mrs. Wiese gently suggested that her son try living in his own apartment, not far away. "But I l-l-like it here," Edison answered, returning to the daily crossword spread out on the kitchen table. His mother had gone into the bathroom to cry — cry because her son hadn't grown up properly, cry because she wouldn't have to lose him as other mothers lose theirs.

The doctors had no answers for why Edison would not grow up properly. He was so late learning to walk that a battery of tests had been ordered. His stuttering had begun on his first day of school. The teachers reported him as "dreamy," "distracted," "gloomy," "slow," but also subject to unaccountable fits of laughter. On intelligence tests he scored so wildly and inconsistently that he was finally exempted from taking them to prevent his skewing the class results. Being held back a grade — a decision vigorously opposed by his father — marked the start of his falling behind his own year, who now had professions, houses, cars, children, divorces. One breakfast, looking up from a book on thermodynamics, he pronounced with a grin, "Better to be an idiot s-s-s-savant than just an idiot." His father had banged his hand on the table and stood up. "You just don't want to grow up, that's your problem," he said, heading down to the basement where he kept his collection of antique barbering equipment, including a reclining chair and striped pole from 1911 that had done service outside a shop in Tuscan, Arizona.

His mother smiled weakly. Perhaps their son was right.

He liked to read Gibbon's *Decline and Fall of the Roman Empire* while watching *Gilligan's Island*. She could see he was upset about his father storming out by the way he was humming "Ode to Joy" under his breath. He looked up and said, "I wish I had lived in P-P-Paris during the Commune. I could have been a waiter to Lafayette." His mother had replied absentmindedly, "Don't be foolish, Edison. I think you could have done a lot better than that."

Now every morning Edison jumps out of bed, brushes his teeth ferociously, stands under an icy shower, shaves most of the bristles from his chin, and puts on the white shirt and black trousers that he insists on wearing even though Beatrice tells him that he has mistaken her place for the dining room of the Ritz. As he creeps down the stairs he can see the blue flicker of his parents' television set, left on while they sleep. He sits in the kitchen eating a bowl of Cocoa Puffs and reading the morning comics.

In the mirrored front hall, Edison puts on his fat winter boots, wool mask, parka. Outside, the sky is a bruise over the houses. Edison kicks the dirty ridge of snow along the sidewalk and hums Schumann's "Kreisleriana." It takes him fifty minutes to reach the last suburban subway stop, where he descends into the earth, from which he will not emerge for another ten hours. At the King Street station he disembarks, taking a series of passageways, escalators, stairs, and revolving doors, passing the still-dark underground shops that line the tunnels beneath the office towers. *Like Aeneas, I descend with courage and fear*, he likes to tell himself.

And this is the extent of the travels that Edison has ventured to make. He is always the first to arrive at the café;

he wears the key that Beatrice finally entrusted him with on a chain under his shirt. So you see: he has not lived, has been nowhere, has experienced almost nothing. What does Edison know about the happiness of human beings? Really, he is a fantastical joke.

And every morning he slides open the glass doors, turns on the espresso machine, puts up the first pot of drip coffee, and begins taking the plastic chairs from the tables. For a moment Edison can almost believe that he is in the café of his imaginings, *refuge of lost souls*.

And then, inevitably, Beatrice arrives.

AT FIVE AFTER NINE, THE crush begins to lessen. Most of the customers are men, senior executive types who can afford to drift into their offices at leisure. Admittedly they look better than the women — *unpummeled* — with their newspapers tucked under their arms and a grim but determined expression on their bluish jaws, as if they are using their full mental powers to keep up the buoyancy of the world's stock exchanges. Here comes one whom Edison has named Mr. Blood because of his tendency to cut himself shaving; as usual there are bits of toilet paper stuck to his chin and neck where he has nicked himself. Ordering his jumbo coffee (*a revolting size; what does he do, soak his feet in it?*), he frowns at the pages of a Canadian Tire catalogue. Peeking, Edison sees a double-page colour spread of lawnmowers.

*Outside the ground is frozen and Mr. Blood dreams of cutting the grass! Like a soldier in the trenches of Verdun who holds on to the memory of life back home. I am a medic behind the front lines, doing inadequate patch-up jobs so that the soldiers can go forth and fight again. Yes, the analogy suits ...*

Mr. Blood leaves a tip, a quarter, which Edison pockets regretfully.

The stream of customers is slower, but steady. Beatrice is fortunate that no Starbucks or Second Cup exists at this turn in the tunnel. As Edison crouches to retrieve a Danish from under the counter, he turns to see her punching the phone buttons. She ought to be calling the bakery for shorting their muffin order this morning. She ought to be finding a new bakery altogether. The pastries look edible enough, with their white glazes and swirls of cherry goop, but they taste like theatrical props. To Edison, who thinks too much about these things, it seems a crime that a customer should bite into one of those sweet consolations and receive a mouthful of sawdust. *Yet another sign of the decline of all civilized values.* But Beatrice makes a hearty profit on them and who is to say the customers are dissatisfied? They never complain, but eat the pastries all the same.

In any case, he knows very well that Beatrice isn't phoning the bakery. She is making her first call of the day to Marcus. Marcus carries a phone on the construction site and so cannot get away from Beatrice's tormenting calls. Edison hears a greeting and looks over the counter to see Alfonso coming up with his mop and pail. His is the first cheerful face that Edison has seen today and the sight of him eases Edison's heart a little.

"One es-p-p-p-resso coming up, Alfonso!"

"I'm no in a hurry. No matter how much I mop, the floor stays wet. People say outside it is snowing."

"Again!"

Edison turns to the machine. As a child he developed the habit of silently addressing inanimate objects around him, from the tube of toothpaste to his bedside lamp. When he bumped into a table he apologized; he patted fire hydrants on the way to school in order to make friends of them so that they wouldn't shift about to confuse him on his way home again. It is a sign of an insufficient maturation that Edison refuses to give up. *When do we stop loving the things around us? Surely there is no moment when we receive proof positive that they do not know of their faithful service to our well-being. It makes no more sense than that we should cease caring for one another*. In like fashion does he address Beatrice's third-hand Gaggia with its antiquated array of levers and valves. The machine is temperamental and Beatrice gave up using it, but Edison has gently persuaded it back into operation. Warmed up, it has impressive steam power and could deliver cup after cup of magnificent espresso, fifty, a hundred at a time, in some flourishing café — Florian's, say, on St. Mark's Square, or Café Reggio in Greenwich Village. But here, alas, there is only Alfonso and his cup.

Edison places the cup on its saucer, with a small spoon and a sugar cube wrapped in paper, a box of which he has purchased himself. He slides it to Alfonso, who has already drawn his hometown Sicilian newspaper from his pocket. Just the sight of the man swirling his spoon does Edison good. He thinks of all this place might be — and is interrupted by Beatrice, screaming into the phone.

"You want us to stay home? On New Year's Eve? I knew it, you don't love me — no, no, admit it! I feel sick. That's right, Marcus, you are making me ill. I might have to phone an ambulance. You swear? Then prove it. Get those tickets. You think it's my fault? Then screw you!"

She slams the receiver. "What did I do?" she wails, picking it up again and frantically hitting the buttons.

*Poor Beatrice. Even the oppressor suffers.*

EDISON MET BEATRICE ON THE evening of his job interview. It was after closing and she was sitting at one of the small round tables, the surface tacky with spilled Coke, lighting up a cigarillo despite the bylaw and flipping through a copy of *People* although there was a sink full of dishes behind the counter, scrunched napkins on the floor, lipsticked cups on the other tables. Immediately Edison took up a broom and began to whisk the debris into the dustpan.

"Eager little beaver, aren't you."

Edison turned crimson. "I've come f-for the job of w-w-w-w-waiter."

"No kidding. Well, it isn't for a waiter. It's for a server. You know the difference? Minimum wage, almost no tips, and you have to do every shit job in the place. Sit down and show me your resumé."

From his pocket, he drew a sheet of paper folded eight times. Beatrice raised an eyebrow and opened it flat on the table. Strands of hair fell into her eyes as she read. "You have something of a checkered career. The number of jobs in which you have lasted for less than a week is impressive."

"I didn't like them."

"What makes you think you'll like this."

"I want to work in a café."

"Uh-huh?" She chain-lit another cigarillo. "You find all this glamorous?"

Vaguely she waved her hand. Edison looked at the chipped counter-top, the fingerprint-marked glass wall separating the café's small space from the tunnel, the cheap plastic furniture, the scrawled *No Credit* sign taped to the cash register. His heart sank. But he said, "I want to s-s-serve people."

"Very commendable. So it's this or the Peace Corps."

Edison laughed, or rather brayed. He didn't disagree. He just said, "People need a b-break."

"You said it." Beatrice inhaled and curled her bottom lip to send a plume of smoke over their heads. "And I'm one of them. Listen, what I need is reliability. Slavish devotion. I've lost three servers in a row. They all went stir-crazy under the ground here, or found better jobs, or couldn't put up with me. You still interested?"

A flashing diamond of light made Edison squint. He saw the reflecting arc of the brass dome on the counter. "Do I get to work the es-s-s-presso m-m-m-machine?"

She narrowed her eyes. "You must have been one of those kids who got a thrill riding in the front of the streetcar. Sure, if you can make the damn thing work. You also get to wash the dishes, take out the garbage, unstop the sink, and throw out customers when they sit too long."

"Throw them out?"

"Suggest they leave. Is that better? Can you use an electronic cash?"

Edison said, "I can start tomorrow."

Beatrice ground out her cigarillo in a dish. Edison noticed

ash on her shirt and marked her for a slovenly nature. When she rose, he jumped up from his chair. She was heavy, her shirt half-tucked in, a rivulet of sweat running above her lip. *This is a tormented soul. Maybe I have been brought here to make her day a little lighter.* He gave a tentative smile.

She looked at him hard. "Don't you try anything. I've got a boyfriend named Marcus and he's built like a stevedore. If you're going to start tomorrow I might as well show you the basics now. This isn't paid time, just so as we're clear. First of all, no long chit-chats with the customers. This is a high turnover business and with the way you t-t-t-talk it'll take ten minutes just to ask about the god-damn weather."

After ten minutes on the microwave, the bagel toaster, the packets of instant hot chocolate, she confessed to him the disaster that was her life. The first marriage gone bad. The abortion. How she was afraid that Marcus too would leave on account of her moods. "I ask too much of him. The guys at work call him pussy-whipped. But if he loved me he'd tell them where to go! If only I could let up. I've tried shrinks, pills. Nothing works. I guess I'm an all-or-nothing personality."

Beatrice lifted a greasy plastic dome from the counter and picked up a slice of carrot cake. She stuffed the front of the wedge into her mouth, leaving a smear of icing on her lip. *How little we can see from the outside of the turmoil within,* he thought. Suddenly she looked at him hard, as if sorry to have opened her mouth. "My advice to you is to start off on the right foot. Be here at 7:30 sharp. Twice late and you're fired."

The next morning was the first and only time that Edison's mother got up with him. "You never took this much trouble to get a decent job," she sighed, watching him from the bathroom door as he stood in his underwear and shaved. "This is a dead end, sweetie. Besides, what if someone we know sees you?" But Edison did not answer. As he pulled on his galoshes she said, "Go. I hope something good comes of it. You're a strange boy." She kissed his forehead, a blessing of sorts.

THE STREAM TOWARDS THE COUNTER diminishes and the customers still arriving stop for a few minutes at the tables to hastily consume their purchases. Edison wipes spilled sugar and cream from the counter, tosses away stir sticks, mourns the absence of spoons. Music from the mall's hidden speakers seeps in, treacly leftover Christmas tunes, overlaid with the more barbaric thumping from the shoe store across the way. Nearby are a tobacco shop, a walk-in dental clinic, a hair salon, a stand with men's ties and, in the passageway, a bench and stunted Ginkgo tree in a pot. *Ersatz outdoors, not a real street at all but a non-place leading to other non-places. What sort of destination is this? We ought to be a warm light in the darkness, a sapphire amidst the dross. But look at us! We are dross ourselves. Disposable. Sham. Without love.*

But even as he wipes, Edison's thoughts are not so hopeless. When he sees the Hand Woman squinting into the café, her breath clouding the glass, he feels a renewal of purpose. *Even something made without proper motive can be a receptacle for good. People have a need. They unknowingly conjure us, and so we are here.* What fantasy and arrogance in unhealthy combination.

The Hand Woman makes sure that Beatrice is not visible before taking a few nimble steps to the nearest table. She gives Edison her scarecrow grin: missing teeth. Edison nods. He calls her the Hand Woman because of the *glorious pathos* of her shawl, stitched like a quilt from dozens of gloves and mittens. During Edison's time it has grown two feet and drags along the ground behind her, the mantle of an exiled queen. At night she sleeps in one of the storage rooms which Alfonso leaves unlocked, an ease to his conscience for throwing out all the others. He always comes in for a fortifying espresso after tossing some bum caught huddling over a heating vent. "Letting in one, okay. But two, ten, a hundred? Is impossible. I lose my job."

Edison peeks into the back room to see Beatrice still on the telephone and then brings the Hand Woman a tuna sandwich and a double-double coffee. Bowing slightly he retreats, Viennese fashion. *A waiter is a true democrat; he treats all patrons the same.* The Hand Woman settles her bulk deeper into the plastic chair, causing the legs to splay, and slurps her coffee.

Mr. Lapidarius comes in.

He drops his enormous case beside his regular table, places his fedora carefully on a chair. To Edison, the sight of Mr. Lapidarius is always welcome. If nothing else, Edison likes the way he sits so pleasantly at his table, as if he, at least, has all the time in the world. Mr. Lapidarius is the café's only regular in the genuine sense, accepting it as a second home. Absolutely bald, with a greenish scalp and impressive eyebrows, he wears the same suit every day, discreetly mended and well-brushed. Now Edison formally presents the menu, which most customers don't know the existence of, but which Mr. Lapidarius scans with interest despite the fact it never changes.

"Thank you, dear boy. I'll have tea and a scone. Have you got Irish Breakfast today?"

Edison's face darkens in shame; he still has not managed to convince Beatrice to buy anything other than discount orange pekoe.

"No matter, friend," Mr. Lapidarius says quickly. "Anything will do. I picked up the tea habit in London, you know. Never been able to get over it. Of course that was forty years ago. I hear they all drink coffee nowadays, like everyone else."

Because Mr. Lapidarius is the only customer who treats the café with respect, Edison always becomes self-conscious in his presence. He warms a small teapot, then puts in the bag and fills the pot with boiling water. Arms tucked in, chin held up, he brings the tray to Mr. Lapidarius's table. The bill is tucked beneath the rim of the cup, for Beatrice demands that customers pay up front.

"Ah, the warmth alone makes one feel jolly, doesn't it?" Mr. Lapidarius says. "I feel expansive today. After all, tonight is New Year's Eve and another year always brings hope for better times. Perhaps you would care to sit for a few minutes?"

"I sh-sh-shouldn't."

"Yes, of course. But a fellow likes a little company now and then."

"Well, I'll ask."

As a matter of principle, Edison believes that waiters ought not to fraternize with customers, but somehow Mr. Lapidarius is different. He pokes his head into the back room where Beatrice is pleading into the telephone.

"I swear I'll never ask you to do anything again. What do you mean, you don't believe me?"

"Pardon me, B-B-Beatrice. May I take my break? Mr. Lap-p-p-pidarius is here."

"What, that Arab? Or is he Greek. All right, but only ten minutes. The salt shakers need filling."

Edison has already replenished them but says nothing, happy to take a seat beside Mr. Lapidarius. "Very companionable," the man says and smiles. "There's no need for me to hurry. It is still too early to begin. I will confide to you a secret of my trade. Never approach people first thing in the morning. They're still in a foul mood for having to get out of bed. It is a salesman's commandment."

"I'm sure you are a v-v-very good salesman," Edison says.

"Well, one mustn't blow one's own trumpet, eh? But it has kept body and soul together all these years. Of course, when I began it was a real profession, even an art form in its small way. Everything's changed, but I'm too old a dog to teach new tricks. Each day I go from office to office, presenting my wares. There are so many buildings and so many floors I never go to the same office twice in six months. My suppliers say that I would do better selling the new gadgets — calculators, pocket video games, electronic calorie counters. But I stick to the old. Pen sets, imitation pearl earrings, watches with hands. Little indulgences, pleasant gifts. I admit lately business has taken something of a downturn, as they say of the stock market, but then I've known too many rises and falls to count. In Cairo, Madrid, San Francisco. Do you know what King Nebuchadnezzar had engraved on his ring? 'All things change.' If times are bad they are sure to get better. And if they are good — well, they are certain to get worse again. In the meantime, one enjoys oneself as one can."

"Yes," Edison says. "I better get back to work. Would you like some hot w-w-w-water?"

"Very kind of you. And you have been good to keep me company. Here, I want to give you something."

He unclasps the latch on his case and takes out a brightly coloured tube on a little cardboard stand, which he places on the table. It looks to Edison like a toy cannon. "This is out of my usual range, but given the date I couldn't resist. You see this fuse? All you need do is light it. In a few seconds a burst of confetti fills the air. So lovely and useless, its only purpose is to make a moment of delight. How is that for a festive New Year? I expect to sell out completely. You take this one."

"Really, I can't."

"You have certain rules. I admire you for it. But this is a gift between friends."

Edison sees a movement out of the corner of his eye, Beatrice stirring in the back room. "I have t-to go!" he says. A moment later he is prying the Hand Woman out of her chair and urging her out of the café.

Turning back again, he sees Beatrice beckoning with a crooked finger from behind the counter. "Was that bag lady trying to come back? That's right, you give her the bum's rush. The last thing customers want is a whiff of that stink. Hey, is that sales guy still hanging over one lousy cup of tea? Go tell him his fifteen minutes is up. Never mind, he's leaving. I don't like the way you arranged those pastries under the counter. It's too goddamn artistic. Mix them up —"

Beatrice stops abruptly and Edison, already moving obediently towards the counter, hears a rasping breath and then a sob. By the time he turns back to her, Beatrice has dissolved into noisy tears.

"Why d-d-don't you sit down?" He risks a hand on her shoulder and she complies as he steers her to a chair. He might have put a consoling arm around her if he didn't fear her taking a swing at him. Instead, he slips behind the counter to spoon some honey into a glass of milk, add a few drops of vanilla, and use the steam spout of the espresso machine to turn the mixture into a warm froth.

"Here, this will m-m-make you feel better."

Beatrice stares at the glass a moment and then took a long draught. "I hate New Year's Eve."

"But why?"

"My first marriage busted up on New Year's. We were in this ballroom with a full swing orchestra. I was wearing a gorgeous silk number with matching pumps, cost me a fortune. We drank a bottle of Moët and when midnight came all these balloons cascaded down, hundreds of them, and the band started playing 'Auld Lang Syne.' We started to dance and Albert said something but it was so noisy I couldn't hear. I kept saying, 'What?' I thought he was trying to tell me that he loved me. But he was really saying, 'I'm leaving you.' I couldn't blame him, the marriage was the shits, but it almost killed me anyway. This time I want it to be different. Marcus keeps asking me to marry him and I keep putting him off just to make sure. I figure that if we can get past the New Year's curse we'll be all right. So I had him book us a table at this classy restaurant, four hundred bucks a couple, Tony Bennett singing, twelve course meal. Then a week ago I got cold feet and told him to cancel. He lost the deposit. Then I changed my mind and made him reserve somewhere else. But then I wasn't sure about that one either. I kept thinking, what if I choose the wrong place? So now tonight is New Year's and we don't have a reservation anywhere. Marcus got fed up and cancelled the last one yesterday and today everybody's booked solid. He says he's too busy to try anymore — they're pouring concrete this morning. He says I've got to stop calling him before he loses his job. I know he's right, it's all my fault, but I can't stop myself. Two minutes ago I phoned again and when he heard my voice he hung up. You see? It's all gone to hell. I'm ruining my own life."

She looks a ruin: eye shadow in rivers down her cheeks, hair dangling limply, blotches forming on her neck. A thought, fully formed, comes to him, which you may judge yourself for its degree of self-delusion. *A waiter who aspires to greatness must make it the sole occupation of his life. That other people should have affairs of the heart is only right. But we are here to be minor players in the dramas of others, not to dwell on our own. It is a sacrifice, but worth everything to make.*

Three silver-haired ladies enter and stand indecisively, trying to choose a table. Perhaps they are senior secretaries forty storeys up, or retirees who like to do their shopping underground. "Push the quiche," Beatrice sniffles. "It's starting to get mushy."

THE FULL LUNCH-HOUR ASSAULT begins, a line of hungry people or, in Edison's mind, a terrifying horde with mouths gaping, *like figures in a painting by Edvard Munch*. They stand four-deep at the counter, shouting their orders, waving office lists. Grabbing the paper bags, they rush out again to get shoes re-heeled, pick up dry cleaning, line up at the pharmacy for Robaxacet, Temazepam, Metamucil, fungicide. He operates the espresso machine and the microwave, Beatrice makes the sandwiches, the tubs of tuna, sliced salami, cheese, jars of mayonnaise and hot mustard placed strategically around the cutting board. For this hour Edison feels them to be comrades almost, and his heart beats fast.

BEATRICE RETREATS ONCE MORE INTO the back. Edison tips the sack of coffee beans into the grinder, gets down on his knees to pick up splotches of egg salad from the floor behind the counter. Only now does he feel the ache in his arms and back.

Rising again, he sees her.

How long has she been sitting there, enveloped in her otter coat? She doesn't look at him but stares out the glass wall into the corridor as Alfonso goes by pushing his mop. A thin band constricts around Edison's chest. He wipes his hands on a towel and comes warily around the counter.

"Hello, m-m-m-Mother."

Mrs. Wiese turns her head, the dense collar brushing her sagging chin. She wears horn-rimmed sunglasses, a Gucci scarf over her hair, violet lipstick. With one leather-gloved hand she removes the sunglasses in order for him to see her reddened eyes.

"Can I get you s-s-something?"

"I never ask you to wait on me at home."

"But s-s-since you're here."

She sighs and drops her glasses into her purse, clamping it shut. "All right. A cappuccino. With just a little chocolate on top, will you, dear?"

Edison almost bows, catching himself in time, and merely returns to the counter. He attempts to operate the machine with his usual precision, but his hand shakes. When he brings over the cappuccino his mother doesn't look at it but drops in three sugar cubes.

"Your father and I want to know if you're coming tonight or not."

"I d-don't know. I haven't had t-t-time to think about it."

"But you know we've been planning this for months. Don't you even want to wish your mother a happy New Year?"

"Of course I do. I just d-don't know —"

"If you've got a better invitation, then just say so."

"I might have to w-w-work."

"Here? They'd bother to keep this place open? What for? Nobody will come, people want to have a good time on New Year's. We've always celebrated together. It wouldn't be the same without you."

"I have r-r-r-r-responsib-b-bilities now."

Mrs. Wiese laughs out loud. *What a brave act she is putting on; I know how much it costs her.* She looks small in the lushness of the otter coat, an anniversary gift from his father that makes her feel uncharacteristically guilty. *Yet she tries to wear it with an air of defiance that exhausts her to keep up.*

"I'm glad you take your job so seriously," she says. "It's just that we know how much you're capable of. I've got to meet your father. He closed the office early to go shopping with me. You know, paper hats, noise makers, cute little gifts. You just have to come. I know there are going to be wonderful things for you in the New Year."

She clasps his hand with her own. She must have had a manicure that morning, as the nails are immaculate. Edison sees the grayish-blue veins pulsing. "I have to g-get back to work. Do you w-want anything else?"

"The cappuccino was delicious, I admit. How much do I owe you?"

She opens her purse again, like a shark's jaws. "It's on the house. I'll t-t-try to come."

She holds his arm as she gets up and kisses gently the corner of his mouth. Edison watches her check her reflection in the glass as she leaves. *Cafés ought to have special mirrors, to make old women look beautiful again.* Cleaning up the table, he sees that she has dropped a glove under the chair. He picks it up and holds it to his face. Chanel Number Five.

BEATRICE JAMS THE RECEIVER INTO its cradle. She emerges from the back room, reaches around Edison to slide open the back of the counter, plunges in her hand, pulls out a jumbo brownie square, and bites ferociously. "He might as well be sticking knives in me, it would hurt just the same.

Look at me — I can't stop eating. Last week I gained a pound and a half. It isn't fair. He doesn't eat like this."

"Perhaps you'd better not," Edison says. He reaches out to take the brownie from her as if it were a loaded gun, but a growl from deep in her throat makes him draw back.

"Has anyone ever had a good New Year's Eve?" she says, mouth full again. "Not just fake good, pretending to have the time of your life. This morning in the car I heard a guy on the radio hoping that everyone's New Year's wish came true. I laughed so hard I almost rear-ended the Saab in front of me. What is my wish? What do I want? Do I want to be with Marcus or never see him again? Suddenly the New Year became a big, monstrous thing, like a mouth wide open that I was driving straight into. Move out of my way."

Her groping hand pulls out a butter tart. "Maybe I'll try to phone again. He's had a few minutes to cool down. Anyway, I can't make it worse."

The half-eaten brownie in one raised hand and the butter tart in the other, she shoehorns past him. In the late afternoon the café is empty and he can see the early trickle of people on the way home. Alfonso appears, carrying the ladder he uses to change the bulbs that flicker in the "antique" lampposts between the benches. He always comes in about now for his second espresso. Edison begins filling the filter basket with grounds.

"So," Alfonso says, motioning with a tilt of his head. "How is the boss today?"

"Lots of phone calls." Edison places the cup, saucer, sugar cube, and small spoon on the counter.

"Don't tell me, man trouble again." He takes his rumpled

paper out of his back pocket and looks down the list of soccer scores. "I think that women, they go nuts on New Year's. Like suddenly they can see all the faults of their men with x-ray glasses. Let's face it, not so many of us can stand up to a close look, you know what I mean? My wife and me, we stay home tonight. After the kids go out, she makes a nice meal and we drink one of my own bottles of wine. Then we go to bed. It's a promise we made way back. We make love on New Year's whether we feel like it or not. That way we know it's at least once a year, eh? And after, if I can't sleep, I go to the basement and work with my lathe. This is what makes a marriage last."

Alfonso tips his cup, wipes his mouth with an oversized handkerchief, and nods his thanks. Passing through the doorway, he comes upon the Hand Woman and moves aside to let her pass. *Like a fortune teller or seer, she moves like some mad Cassandra bearing news no one wants to hear.* Not seeing Beatrice about, she sits at her regular table. Edison heaps a bowl with pre-cut fruit salad, giving off a slight odor of preservative, and places it before her. The Hand Woman clutches the spoon and raises a ball of honeydew to her mouth. She too has a smell, a potent combination of earth and old wine. Her hair is braid-like, her chin marked by a scaly rash. He remembers the leather glove that his mother left behind and, pulling it from his back pocket, holds it out to her.

"Perhaps you c-c-can use this?"

The Hand Woman takes it from him, sniffing suspiciously and then rubbing it against her cheek. She fishes up the end of her shawl and places it against a gap between a woolen mitt and a ski glove. "A good fit," she says, nodding. It is the first time he has heard her surprisingly girlish voice. From somewhere among her folds she pulls out a needle and thread and gets to work.

Back behind the counter, Edison takes advantage of the quiet to eat a sandwich. As he often does at such a moment, he permits himself the pleasure of imagining how the café might be. *If only it were a true refuge of the spirit, a window upon the passing human scene; a place where patrons might read, speak to one another, sit in public anonymity, poetic reverie, or deep melancholy. Where they could ponder, draw, work out elaborate algebraic equations, write novels or letters. A café welcoming to rich, poor, the thinker on the verge of a breakthrough, the sexually disappointed …*

His reverie is interrupted by the appearance of an aggressively groomed young man: hair slicked and combed back from the shallow forehead, one understated earring loop, silk tie, and red suspenders, but no jacket. "Hang on a minute," he says into his cellphone. And to Edison: "You ought to install a fax. Then I could send our order down and not have to wait. We're doing a presentation. Sure, the food was my call, but who knew they'd eat so much?"

Edison suppresses a grimace and takes the list from the man. He begins filling a shallow box with Danishes and cups of coffee. The man pockets his change, tucks the phone under his ear, and picks up the box. "Yeah, I'm on my way up. Start the overheads."

Edison tries to slip back into his thoughts. He is just warming up with *chess boards* and *international newspapers on wooden dowels* when he hears a scream.

He looks up to the sight of flying Danishes and fountains of coffee spiralling in the air. Evidently the Hand Woman had monumentally risen from her chair and the young man in suspenders had run straight into her. Now the young man dances about swearing, pulling his steaming shirt from his skin. Edison is already scooping up towels when Beatrice barrels past from the back room. She grabs the Hand Woman by the shoulders. "Vermin! Slut! Get out!" Leaning over the counter, she grabs two fistfuls of change from the register and hurls them. Quarters, nickels, dimes pelt the Hand Woman, ricochet off the glass walls, spin about the floor.

Hunched over to protect herself, the Hand Woman shuffles down the corridor.

The young man says, "I'm a dead man. They've been looking for a noose just like this to hang around my neck."

AT TEN MINUTES TO SIX the shoe store closes its door, followed by the dental office, tobacco shop, hair salon, and tie stand. The stream towards the subway surges one last time and then slowly lessens. Edison dampens a rag and begins to wipe down the tables and chairs. In a moment Beatrice will emerge to clean out the till and warn him to lock up properly.

*I've read too many books. Who knows what people want? A job is a job, that's all.*

He gives up trying to remove a coffee stain on a table, something he would never have done before, and slouches back to the counter to lean there and do absolutely nothing. But Beatrice springs from the back room, startling him with her whoop of joy. "We're going, we're going! Marcus got tickets to the construction workers' ball. He had to pay a fortune and he did it for me. He must adore me, otherwise he wouldn't have. I feel faint. My God, what time is it? I've got to go home and peel my face. Just leave everything and close up, all right? You can go any time."

If he went home now his mother and father would make him help decorate for the party. "I'm n-not in any rush," he says. "I might clean up a b-bit."

"Whatever," Beatrice mumbles, buttoning her coat. "But I'm not paying you for the time."

"You have a great night, Beatrice."

"God, I hope so. Maybe the New Year will find me a way out of this subterranean dump. I could sell it. You seem to like it here. Wouldn't be interested in taking over the lease, would you? Stupid question I guess, on the salary I pay you. Just think, in two hours I'll be on the dance floor!" She reaches up to kiss Edison on the cheek. "You have a great New Year's. And close up soon. There ain't going to be any business. You spend too long in this joint as it is."

Beatrice is right about business. The doors of the underground mall are kept open for the subway entrance and now, when anyone passes, Edison can see a flash of satin or a black trouser cuff beneath the hem of a winter coat. He only has to summon the energy to close up and make his way home, but a weariness has come over him and he wants only to lean his head on the counter and close his eyes. There is no more thumping music, just the whirring of an overhead fan. A couple, arm-in-arm, notice the lights on and peer in curiously as they go by. *They feel pity for me, I see it in their smiles. I give them someone to look down on.*

Edison begins wiping out the microwave.

At half past eight he undoes the top button of his white shirt and turns off the espresso machine. He is putting a chair up on its table when a tap on the glass makes him look up. Mr. Lapidarius, holding his salesman's case in one hand and his fedora in the other. His bald head half in shadow.

"Of course you are closing," he said, coming round to the entrance.

"No," Edison says, putting the chair back again. He flicks the switch on the espresso machine, catching his reflection which reminds him to redo the top button of his shirt. Mr. Lapidarius eases into the chair, sighs deeply, and places his hat on the table. "A most discouraging day. Perhaps you can make me something a little special."

"How ab-b-bout an espresso mocha con panne?"

"Con panne?"

"Whipped cream."

"Sounds just like what the doctor ordered."

"Coming right up."

"A shame you don't have a radio. We could listen to some dance music appropriate to the evening. I was rather a good dancer in my youth. I remember doing the tango once with the wife of the second assistant to the ambassador from Brazil. Ah well, that is a long time ago. Memories, my friend, they save us and persecute us."

Edison uses a tall glass, working diligently at the machine, piling a turret of whipped cream on top. He carries the drink on a tray along with the only long spoon in the café. Mr. Lapidarius takes an experimental taste and delivers the verdict with a grateful smile. "This is balm for the soul. There was a time when people took pride in their work as you do. But now? Does anyone know how to enjoy himself? The lexicographers will have to remove the word 'gaiety' from the dictionary. Do you know how many confetti cannons I sold? Three. There is no more room for the exquisitely frivolous moment. Tomorrow I will spend the first day of the New Year consulting an atlas for a new destination. I have enthusiasm for nothing more. Perhaps you would care to sit down for a while?"

"I'm s-s-sorry," Edison says. "But now I'm the only one on duty."

"I understand."

PERHAPS THE SALESMAN HAS FALLEN asleep, or is just resting; in any case, he doesn't move from his chair, not even to uncross his arms. As long as he is there, Edison feels obliged to stay open, and makes sure not to disturb him as the hands of the oversized clock pass nine-thirty, ten.

He hears a woman's clicking heels before he sees her in the passageway. Edison raises his eyebrows; it is the Wasp, who every morning fights her way to the counter without speaking a word. Now her face looks more gaunt, even jaundiced, the mouth drawn further downwards, as she hesitates at the entrance and looks first at the salesman and then the waiter. Instead of the tightly belted skirt, she wears a bare-shouldered dress with a spiral of glittering sequins. Her stockings, too, shimmer as she darts to the table farthest from Mr. Lapidarius, perching on a chair as if it were unclean or might collapse. Edison waits a beat before making his solemn approach.

"Do you have any liquor?" She does not look up.

"I am s-sorry, Madame. This is not a bar."

"Damn."

"We do, however, have a bottle of c-cognac which the proprietess sometimes adds to her own coffee."

"Bring me one like that." She gives him a dark glare.

"Very good."

A healthy person would avoid such a look, or even return it in kind. But Edison only draws it in, as if to extract some poison from the woman. *Someone not a true waiter might be injured by those glaring eyes. But my profession demands an acceptance of such psychological displacements. Who or what has made her so miserable I cannot know, but that I should serve as a stand-in is a fate to which I uncomplainingly submit. Hate me and feel better.*

Edison himself feels a little light-headed, perhaps from the sound of his newly stirred inner voice or the mere aroma of the cognac. He puts the cup down on her table by a folded napkin. Immediately the Wasp takes a long swallow; she makes an appreciative sound, like the sigh of one descending into a hot bath. But Edison has no time to linger, for he hears a sort of flapping of enormous wings and turns to see the Hand Woman fluttering her shawl in the doorway. Perhaps fearing that Beatrice is about, she displays herself peacock-fashion. Seeing only Edison, she lets the shawl fall to her shoulders again and, smiling, takes her regular seat. Then she waggles her fingers at him.

Edison stares; she has never called him over before. An instant later he stands dutifully by her side. "May I help you?"

"What's the drink called with the foam on top."

"Cappuccino."

"No, I mean whipped cream."

"That's a Viennese coffee."

She looks up at him and he notices a few wiry hairs growing from her nostrils and chin. *But her eyes, her hazel eyes, must have been beautiful when she was young. At least to somebody.*

"I'd like to try one of those."

"With p-pleasure."

He hunts under the sink for another real glass, washes it, and makes the coffee. By the time he sets it down on her table the whipped cream is beginning to melt into pale swirls in the coffee below. She picks up the glass with both hands, nails blackened, and puts it to her mouth. When she put it down again a spot of whipped cream clings to her nose.

"Do you like it?"

She ruminates on the question, making a chewing motion with her mouth. "Well," she says finally, "it doesn't disappoint."

OUTSIDE, EDISON IMAGINES, THE DARK of night is changing: growing deeper. But here, in this little underworld, beneath the weight of sixty-three storeys it is always the same, as if time does not exist. Edison's two patrons sit in their chairs as if in an airport waiting lounge, their flights eternally delayed. *What a shame I can't do more for them. Ah, fool. Know your limitations. A waiter provides solace; he can't heal.*

Someone deliberately clears his throat behind Edison. He sees three men in dark coats, bunched in the doorway as if holding on to one another. They are dressed identically —

Edison can see dark trouser cuffs and patent leather shoes — but otherwise are in no way alike. As Edison approaches, the gangly one says, "Open, are you?"

"Yes, w-we are."

"That's lucky. You wouldn't happen to know of a private office party around here? Name of Mecklinger."

"I'm afraid not."

"That's a shame. We must have got the wrong floor. Or building. Or name."

"Or year," says the short one.

"Whatever the reason, it puts us at rather loose ends. We were counting on the hors d'oeuvres," says the rotund one.

"I can make you s-s-sandwiches," Edison says.

"That would do very well." Only as the three file in does Edison see the battered instrument cases that had been hidden behind them. At the table they remove their coats, revealing bow ties and tails. Edison is already working on their double-decker sandwiches, and when he returns the trio fall upon them ravenously.

WHEN A MAN AND WOMAN with an infant arrive at eleven p.m., Edison is no longer surprised. By now it seems almost natural that people should be wandering about, looking for somewhere to take shelter from the inevitable disappointments of this night. The man looks familiar, but it takes Edison a moment to identify him as Mr. Blood without the toilet paper bits. The woman he also recognizes; she, too, is among the morning crush, or used to be, for he hasn't seen her in some months. He could not remember the two of them ever speaking or even looking at one another, yet here they are with this bond sleeping in the woman's arms, mouth open and nose encrusted. Mr. Blood holds the diaper bag. They sit at the table beside the Hand Woman, whom he acknowledges with a reserved nod.

Edison bends towards them, speaking in a whisper so as not to wake the child. "Would you c-care for s-something?"

"Do you have hot cider?" the mother asks. Mr. Blood looks away.

"Certainly. And — perhaps some warm m-m-milk?"

"No, that's all right. I've got my own."

"Of course."

He sees the woman try to take Mr. Blood's hand, who pulls away from her.

Returning with the ciders, Edison hears the opening bars of a Schubert waltz. The three musicians have taken out their instruments — violin, viola, cello — and now play softly, so as not to wake the baby. They do not play well, but their presence is fortunate, adding as it does a kind of soundtrack to the accumulated coincidences of the night. Crowded between the table and the counter, the musicians elbow one another as they bow, whispering insults under their breath. But to Edison they are a sweet accompaniment to the clinking of glasses and spoons.

The baby wakes, a sudden wail. The woman puts it to her breast, where the infant struggles before settling down.

WHEN THE CLOCK READS TWELVE minutes to midnight, only Edison appears to take notice. *The earth spins, the year reaches its end, we are propelled into the future even without knowing.*

More orders come from the tables, a lively atmosphere

prevails, and Edison moves with that quick dance-like step peculiar to waiter with a full house. He is carrying a tray of lemonade (refreshment for the musicians, compliments of Mr. Lapidarius) when a woman hurls herself into the café and halts just short of colliding with him. She has a rather horsey face (*that is, if a horse can look as if it is in agony*) and wears a dress like a flapper. Even as she is making her apologies, Edison can see behind her the Wasp slowly rise from her chair. The first woman must have sensed her presence, for she turns around and the two looked at one another with — what? *Fury, alarm, hope, desire; there are no emotions they do not experience.*

"My God," Mr. Lapidarius calls out in mock exasperation. "If you're not going to embrace one another then at least dance!"

Everyone laughs, if hesitantly. The two women, suddenly embarrassed, laugh too. They do embrace, after which they start to dance quite gracefully. Edison puts down the lemonades and, having no call for his service, surveys the café before him. He sees the Hand Woman smiling in her chair, Mr. Blood impulsively reaching over to take the hand of the woman nursing the baby, the women dancing, Mr. Lapidarius acknowledging the thanks of the musicians. It must be admitted that something unusual is occurring, not likely to repeat itself, allowing Edison to feel that nothing needs to be different from the way it is.

And then he sees them.

Mr. and Mrs. Wiese.

They are staring into the café, hunched in their twin fur coats. They lean so close that their breath makes clouds on the glass wall. Edison moves between the tables to meet them at the entrance.

"We left our party to come and get you," Mrs. Wiese says. "It wasn't much fun. We worried that you were here all by yourself."

"It turns out we are q-q-quite busy."

Mr. Wiese says, "We looked around and realized that the others didn't matter."

For the first time, Edison realizes how much he looks like his father. He says, "I c-can't go anywhere. I have to look after these p-people."

"Then we'll stay," his mother says. "Look after us, too. We brought some champagne."

His father hefts the paper bag in his hands with an over-sized bottle inside. Edison says, "All the tables are taken."

"A string trio." His father moves his head to the tempo. "But you're right. There's no room, Florence. We'll go."

"Excuse me."

It was Mr. Lapidarius, who has risen from his seat. "If you are looking for a place, I am all by myself. You are welcome to join me at my table."

His mother looks over her glasses at him. "How gallant. But we don't want to impose."

"No, stay," Edison says. *Here I am a waiter but if I must also be a son, then so be it.* He pulls out their chairs and, making his usual bow, heads back to the counter with the bottle of champagne.

Edison hears a loud popping sound. Confetti and stream-ers rain over their heads. "Happy New Year!" shouts Mr. Lapidarius. He lights another paper cannon, a third.

"Happy New Year," people call to each other. There is much shaking of hands and even kisses.

Using the proper technique, Edison turns not the cork but the champagne bottle; there is another *pop* and everyone applauds.

THE MUSICIANS PLAY, THE CHAMPAGNE is drunk, the dancers move across the floor. Not until after two do they begin to leave: first Mr. Blood and the mother and baby, then the Wasp and the flapper. Mr. and Mrs. Wiese linger at the entrance, while she tries and fails to speak. Edison kisses her on each cheek and sends them home. Mr. Lapidarius helps the musicians pack up. "A good New Year to you, my friend," he says, clasping Edison's hand with emotion.

Edison cleans the tables and sweeps the floor. He turns off the espresso machine and then the lights. He slides shut and locks the glass door. When he enters the corridor of the mall it is deserted. Instead of heading straight to the subway, he rides the escalator up to the lobby of the office building where a guard has fallen asleep at the vast marble desk behind which blink the changing images of the security camera screens. Edison crosses to the revolving doors, pauses a moment (they always make him dizzy) and pushes his way out.

The events of this night are so unlikely that they might as well never have happened. It is true that such exceptions to the general run of things can sometimes do more harm than good. However, let no more be said on that theme. As Edison emerges onto the sidewalk, the lightest possible snow is falling. The soreness in his heart unfolds, flutters into the dark sky, and then comes back to rest inside him once more. In a few hours the sun will rise over the New Year. Edison will go home and sleep the humble sleep of a waiter. And then he will return. The café must open again, for people must have somewhere to go.

# Acknowledgements

"The Floating Wife" was first published in *The Antigonish Review*.

"Shit Box," "My Life among the Apes," and "Dreyfus in Wichita" were first published in *Taddle Creek*. The quotation in "Dreyfus in Wichita" is from Richard D. Mandell, *Paris 1900*, University of Toronto Press, 1967. Used by permission.

"Wolf," under the title "Berlin," was first published in *Grain*.

"The Creech Sisters" was first published in *The Fiddlehead* and *Best Canadian Stories 00*.

"The Little Underworld of Edison Wiese" was first published in a limited edition by Hungry I Books. It is dedicated to Susan Matoff.

Thanks to Bernard Kelly and Rebecca Comay for their close readings of these stories. And to the journal editors who offered valuable suggestions: Conan Tobias, Norman

Ravvin, Dave Margoshes, and Richard Cumyn. And finally to Marc Côté and the crew at Cormorant.

I am grateful for the financial support of the Ontario Arts Council and the Toronto Arts Council.